THE INSURANCE MAN

CRAIG HOPPER

This book is a work of fiction. Any resemblance to actual persons, living or dead, or actual events or locales is entirely coincidental.

It is sincerely hoped that the 3rd Battalion, Parachute Regiment and its veterans of the Falklands conflict are not offended by anything in this book.

Cover Design: Craig Hopper

ACKNOWLEDGMENTS

Thank you to my initial readers Lesley, Laura, John, Stefan and Rob for your time, feedback and suggestions. Your help is very much appreciated.

Also, thank you to my friend, colleague and fellow author, Wayne Clark, for listening, for our conversations, your advice and tips.

Finally, thank you to Lauren for final proof reading and a great job with editing.

THANK YOU GEORGE FINEGAN

PROLOGUE

London - 4:30pm Friday 25th June 2010

The young Personal Assistant behind the glass-topped desk put the telephone down and looked over at Blowers, who was sitting and thumbing through a home and lifestyle magazine. She smiled and said loudly, "Mr Fitch will see you now."

Blowers noticed that she had dimples when she smiled. He smiled back and rose from the soft, leather sofa. He fastened the middle button of his suit jacket and smiled again at the young woman.

"This way," she indicated with her left hand as she rose behind her desk.

Blowers noticed that she had long, slender fingers, perfectly manicured fingernails and was not wearing an engagement or wedding ring.

The Personal Assistant stepped from behind the desk and began walking down the soft, carpeted corridor towards some deep red mahogany double doors. She was tall and slender and Blowers guessed that she was five feet seven inches tall without the two-inch heels she was wearing. He followed two steps behind and watched how the grey, tight, hugging pencil skirt made the young woman take short steps and gave her a wiggle as she walked. A woman who looks after herself and has exquisite taste, Blowers thought to himself.

She stopped at the doors, knocked twice and then pushed them both open. "Please," she again indicated with her left hand for Blowers to enter the office.

Blowers smiled and said "Thank you," and he entered the office of Albert Fitch, CEO of Fitch Speciality Insurance.

"You're welcome," and she winked at him.

"Now now Jenny, stop flirting with Mr Blowers and please reschedule all my remaining meetings for today. Thank you," Fitch said with a slight hint of a Welsh accent from behind his antique mahogany desk.

The assistant nodded, "Of course Mr Fitch."

Blowers winked at the young woman and she smiled as she closed the doors behind her. He felt the deep pile of the carpet under his feet and he looked around the office. He was impressed by its decadence; old paintings hung on the wall, a china dinner service in the rosewood cabinet, sporting trophies on the shelf.

Fitch watched Blowers and waved his hand around the room. "Just a few trinkets I've picked up from here and there." He pointed at the high-backed leather chair just to the right of his desk, "Please sit Mr Blowers."

Blowers stepped over to the chair, leaned over the desk and offered his right hand for a handshake.

Fitch stood, fastened the middle button of his suit jacket and firmly shook the offered hand.

Blowers noticed the diamond encrusted ring on Fitch's right wedding finger.

Fitch caught Blowers glance at the wedding ring and explained, "I'm Orthodox Christian." He again indicated to the chair, "Please sit Mr Blowers."

Blowers unbuttoned his suit jacket and sat. He sank into the soft leather and immediately felt comfortable.

Fitch immediately got down to business, "When you telephoned this morning, my assistant said that you were most insistent to speak with me this afternoon. Have you got some good news for me Mr Blowers?"

Blowers reached into his right inside jacket pocket, pulled out a long, slender, black velvet necklace box and handed it to Fitch.

Fitch turned the box over in his hands, opened it, smiled and then snapped it shut. He put the box down on the red, leather, writing mat in front of him, leaned back in his chair and smiled. "The DeMartin diamonds. We were about to pay out for their loss."

Blowers nodded, "I believe you were."

Fitch leaned forward and tapped the necklace box with his right index finger. "How did you find them?"

Blowers reached again into his right inside jacket pocket and pulled out a photograph. He handed it to Fitch. "That photograph was taken at a charity dinner in San Francisco for US veteran soldiers a week ago. The lady on the right in the midnight blue dress is my wife and on her right..."

Fitch cut in and finished the sentence. "And on her right, is Madame Isabella DeMartin wearing the diamonds she claimed were stolen."

"Yes" Blowers confirmed, "She's not a very bright lady."

Fitch looked at Blowers and then again at the photograph. "You're married to Faith Roberts, the supermodel?"

"Yes." Blowers smiled. He could see that Fitch was impressed.

Fitch handed the photograph back to Blowers. "You're a lucky man," he grinned. He continued, "How did you come about the necklace?"

"Legally," Blowers confirmed. "And Madame DeMartin understands that in exchange for her not being prosecuted for insurance fraud, that you will keep the necklace."

Fitch was pleased and slapped the desk. "Quite so," he said loudly.

Blowers stood up and fastened the middle button of his suit jacket. "I think our business is concluded Mr Fitch," and he took out a card from his breast pocket. "Fifty- thousand pounds into the bank account on the card if you please."

Fitch took the card but did not look at it. He held out his right hand. "Our business is indeed concluded Mr Blowers."

Blowers firmly shook Fitch's hand, turned and walked towards the mahogany double doors. They opened before he reached them and he smiled at Fitch's Personal Assistant as he walked through. "Good day miss," he said happily.

She smiled back. "Have a nice evening Mr Blowers."

Blowers began whistling 'happy days are here again' as he walked down the corridor towards the lifts to leave Fitch's offices.

Home Farm, Barnard Castle, County Durham - 8:00am Saturday 8th December 2012

There was a bang, a flash and sudden screaming. Blowers sat up with a start and opened his eyes. He was sweating. He rubbed his face, focused and looked around the room. He realised that he was safe and let out a long sigh. He stretched his arms above his head and groaned as his back and shoulders stretched.

The study was cold; the fire in the hearth had gone out in the early hours of the morning, but bright sunlight was starting to stream into the room through the half open curtains. He squinted as his eyes got used to the bright morning light and he rubbed his face again.

There was movement in the kitchen, feet shuffling, running water and cups clinking. The smell of frying bacon and sausages was wafting into the study and Blowers suddenly felt hungry. He stretched again and scratched his head.

Blowers' back was stiff. He had slept in the old recliner again; the third time this week. He listened to the sounds coming from the kitchen and then there was hissing and screeching outside of the study door.

A black and white cat ran into the room and jumped onto his knee. Blowers stroked the cat and it immediately began purring.

He spoke to the cat. "Good morning Napoleon. Has Wellington been kicking your arse again?" The cat continued purring.

A grey tabby cat walked into the room with an air of arrogance about it, sat down on the hearth rug and began preening.

"Wellington!" Blowers said sharply.

The cat looked up.

"Leave Napoleon alone."

The cat ignored Blowers and resumed its preening.

Blowers continued to stroke Napoleon. He did not want to move because these were peaceful calming moments away from his nightmares.

An old female voice shouted from the kitchen "Mr Blowers, your breakfast is ready."

Blowers pushed the cat off his knee, yawned and stretched again.

He stiffly got up from the recliner, left the study and followed the smell of cooked bacon and sausages down the hallway and into the kitchen.

A fire was roaring in the hearth and the heat of the room hit him.

"Good morning Mr Blowers," the old lady said happily. "It's a lovely bright sunny winter's morning."

"Good morning Mrs Pitt," Blowers returned politely and sat down in his place at the head of the old oak kitchen table.

Two places were set at the table and Blowers watched the old lady serve up the cooked breakfast. She put a plate of fried food down in front of him and then sat down at the place setting with her plate. The housekeeper smiled at Blowers. "Eat up. My old mam used to say that you can't have a good day if you don't have a good breakfast inside you."

Blowers cut into a sausage, dipped it into the fried egg yolk and put it into his mouth. It tasted good.

"What have you got planned for today?" the old lady asked.

Blowers swallowed a mouthful of fried bread. "I'm going to Oxford with Davy to see a man about an XR 2."

Mrs Pitt looked blankly at him.

"It's an old Ford Fiesta. A sporty version," he explained.

"Oh! Lovely," and the old lady stuffed a piece of sausage into her mouth.

Blowers smiled at his housekeeper's ignorance about cars and took a drink of coffee.

"How's the car restoration business going with young Davy Passmoor?"

Blowers swallowed a mouthful of egg and took another drink of coffee. "Very well. He's a very talented mechanic and he works hard. We've already got twelve Ford cars ready to be sold."

"It's a good thing you're doing; helping him out like this," Mrs Pitt said sincerely.

"What do you mean?" Blowers was puzzled by the old lady's remark.

Mrs Pitt put her knife and fork down on her plate. "Oh! Him having a wife and a little lass to support and there not being much work around at the moment."

Blowers became irritated. "You mean, Mrs Pitt, that nobody would give him a job because of his family name and their reputation for illegal gambling, extortion and murder."

The old lady looked at the table. "Yes," she said quietly.

Blowers realised he had spoken too sharply to the old lady and apologised. He continued, "Davy's a good lad. He's kept his nose clean while I've known him and as I have said, he has a talent for fixing up old cars. I trust him Mrs Pitt."

The old lady said nothing and took a bite out of a slice of toast.

Blowers took a big gulp of coffee and cursed himself for making his housekeeper feel foolish.

There was a long silence as Blowers and the housekeeper continued with their breakfast.

Blowers broke the silence. "You're a lovely lady Mrs Pitt. You're just the person to keep me on the straight and narrow."

The old lady smiled.

Blowers continued. "I don't know what I'd do without you."

Mrs Pitt nodded. "Well, I best get on. There's lots to do," she announced as she rose from the table to take her plate away to the kitchen sink.

Blowers got up from the table and announced, "I'm going to take a shower."

Mrs Pitt set about clearing away the dishes from the table.

Blowers went upstairs and entered his bedroom. He took off his jumper and shirt and threw them onto a pile of dirty clothes in a corner of the room. It was cold and he shivered. He then unbuckled his belt and took off his jeans, leaving them on the floor where he was standing. He took off his socks and boxer shorts and threw them onto the same pile of dirty clothes as the shirt and jumper. The varnished wood floor was cold under foot and he walked quickly into the bathroom for a shower.

As Blowers was turning on the shower taps, Mrs Pitt was watching a grey Range Rover come up the lane, enter the cobbled farmyard and stop about twenty feet away from the farmhouse door.

"Mr Blowers is not going to like this," she said to Napoleon the cat, as he rubbed himself around her ankles and purred.

She dried her hands on her apron and opened the old farmhouse door. Cold winter air rushed into the kitchen. She watched a dark-haired man in a dark grey, tailored top coat get out of the car.

The stranger was tall and walked with a straight back. His hair was slicked neatly back; the knot of his deep red tie was perfect and his black oxford shoes were highly polished.

"Smells like money and trouble," the old housekeeper said to herself.

The stranger walked over to her and said with a smile, "Good morning. My name is Albert Fitch and I'm looking for Mr Andrew Blowers."

Mrs Pitt crossed her arms and said sternly, "Nobody of that name lives here mister."

Fitch peered past the old lady into the kitchen. "I was told that he does." He was still smiling.

"Well I'm telling you he doesn't," Mrs Pitt said sharply.

Fitch was still smiling. "And your name is?"

The old housekeeper's face began to redden with anger. "None of your bloody business. Now get lost." She turned, walked into the kitchen and slammed the old oak door shut.

Fitch laughed out loud. The landlord at the Red Lion pub had told him that he would have to get past the 'old battle-axe' first. He knocked on the door. Nobody answered. He knocked again and still no answer.

Flurries of snow began to fall and Fitch was getting cold, so he retreated to the Range Rover to wait.

Blowers savoured the hot water running over his body. He closed his eyes and began to imagine that Faith was in the shower with him. He could feel her hands gently moving across his shoulders and her breath in his ear as she whispered, "I love you." The memory of her still cut through him like a knife and he began to cry. He slid down the tiled wall until he was sat with his legs pulled tight up against his chest. He sobbed uncontrollably.

When Blowers entered the kitchen, he found Mrs Pitt with her hands on her hips and staring out of the kitchen window and across the farmyard.

"He's still out there," she announced.

Blowers looked out of the window. "Who's out there?"

"A man by the name of Fitch," she hissed.

Blowers was instantly irritated. "Fuck! How'd he find me?" he asked himself.

"It'll be that bugger at the Red Lion who'll have told him you live here," Mrs Pitt said with disdain.

"Now, now, Mrs Pitt," Blowers said sarcastically.

The old lady turned and glared at Blowers.

Blowers held his hands up in defence. "Okay! It'll be that bugger at the Red Lion who told him where I live." He began laughing and Mrs Pitt hit him with a tea towel.

The housekeeper turned back to the window. "Who is he?"

"The ghost of Christmas past," Blowers said grimly.

"What does he want?"

Blowers sighed. "He probably wants me to find some stolen jewels, an old painting, or a priceless vase. Who the hell knows?"

Mrs Pitt pointed at the Range Rover parked in the farmyard. "He knows."

Silence descended upon the kitchen as Blowers and the old housekeeper stared out of the window at the car parked in the farmyard.

After a couple of minutes staring through the window at the Range Rover, Blowers sighed and said, "I suppose I should go out and see what he wants."

"I suppose you should," Mrs Pitt replied without taking her eyes off the parked car.

Fitch finished his phone call and put the phone back in the holder attached to the dashboard. He looked out of the tinted, front passenger-side window and saw two faces looking out at him through the kitchen window. He smiled to himself; Andrew Blowers was there. He looked at his watch, nine thirty am, and then back at the farmhouse.

The farmhouse door opened and Blowers was walking across the farmyard towards the car. Fitch pressed a button on the door panel and the front passenger-side window lowered. He noticed that Blowers had lost a lot of weight, which was not surprising since the death of his wife.

Blowers was annoyed that Fitch had found him and when he reached the car he said sharply, "What do you want Mr Fitch?"

"Good morning Mr Blowers. You've been a hard man to find," Fitch said smiling.

Blowers was getting impatient. "Enough of the pleasantries. What do you want?"

Fitch's face turned serious. "I was hoping that you would agree to find a stolen diamond tiara for me."

"No."

"There's a five percent finder's fee," Fitch teased.

Blowers became curious. "How much is the tiara worth?"

"It's insured with us for five-million pounds," Fitch said matter of factly.

Blowers pushed his hands deep into the pockets of his reefer jacket and hunched his shoulders against the cold, north wind and the flurries of snow. He quickly did the maths; a two-hundred and fifty thousand pounds job. He kicked at the cobbles with his boots and looked Fitch dead in the eyes. "I'll do it. I'll meet you in your office at eleven am tomorrow morning to discuss the details of the case." With that, Blowers turned and walked quickly back to the farmhouse.

Fitch pressed the button on the door panel and the window rose. He let out a long, slow, breath of relief. Blowers was his last hope for finding the tiara or in two weeks' time, he would be paying out five-million pounds in insurance money to Baroness Cardenham.

Mrs Pitt was waiting in the doorway with her arms folded across her chest.

"I'm back in the insurance game," Blowers announced as he walked past her and into the kitchen. As he walked down the hallway to go upstairs and pack a bag of clothes and personal items, he heard his housekeeper slam the farmhouse door shut.

Oxford - 4:00pm Saturday 8th December

Blowers turned the Range Rover onto Belbroughton Road and began looking through the darkness for a house called Balnagowan. He found it easily because a red XR 2 was parked on the driveway. He pulled the Range Rover and trailer over to the kerbside, turned off the engine and got out of the car. He pulled the collar of his reefer jacket up around his ears to block the cold, winter wind and pushed his gloved hands deep into the coat's pockets.

Davy Passmoor got out of the passenger side of the Range Rover and shone a large torch over the XR 2. "It looks in good condition, Andrew," he said nodding at the car.

"We'll see," Blowers answered flatly. "You look around the bodywork, Davy and I'll speak to the owner, Mr. Brown."

"Aye, okay." Davy made his way over to the car to begin his inspection.

Blowers walked up the garden path but before he reached the door, it opened. A tall bald headed man wearing fashionably faded jeans and an old faded sweatshirt stepped out into the cold, dark evening and walked down the path towards him.

Blowers held out his right hand. "Mr Brown. I'm Andrew Blowers. I've come to see about buying your XR 2"

Mr Brown firmly shook Blowers hand. "Of course. We spoke on the phone yesterday. I saw the light being shone on the car and I thought it might be you."

Blowers turned to look at the car and nodded towards it. "It looks in nice condition."

"Had her since new. I'll be sad to see her go," Mr Brown said with some fondness in his voice.

Blowers and Mr Brown watched Davy look painstakingly around the car. Mr Brown broke the silence. "She's in tip-top condition and a bargain at five-thousand pounds."

Blowers turned to Mr Brown. "I'll let Davy decide that after he's finished having a good look around and been for a test drive."

Mr Brown nodded. "Of course. I'll get you the keys."

Davy walked over to Blowers and nodded back at the car. "The bodywork and underneath are in good condition. I need to see how she drives though."
Mr Brown returned with the keys and handed them to Davy.

Davy smiled and said, "Thanks." He turned and walked over to the car.

"Cup of tea?" Mr Brown asked Blowers.
Blowers nodded. "Yes. Thanks," and the two men went into the house.

Twenty minutes later Davy drove the XR 2 onto Mr Brown's driveway. He switched off the engine. "Nice," he said to himself. He again quickly looked around the interior of the car and then got out and walked up to the house. As he reached the door, it opened.

"A nice motor Mr Brown. She's been well looked after," Davy said with a smile.

Mr Brown turned to Blowers. "I believe that your mechanic has declared that we have a deal at five-thousand pounds."

Blowers smiled. "I guess we do Mr Brown," and he reached into the inside pocket of his reefer jacket for a white envelope filled with fifty-pound notes.

Mr Brown quickly counted the money and then shook Blowers hand. "A pleasure doing business with you Mr Blowers," he grinned.

Davy drove the XR 2 onto the trailer and then got into the front passenger seat of the Range Rover.

Blowers turned to him. "I'll drive to the station and then you can take the XR 2 back to the farm."

"Where are you going?" Davy asked.

"To London to see a man about a missing diamond tiara," and he started the engine.

Davy was puzzled by the answer but didn't bother to ask for an explanation. He turned the radio on instead.

London - 8:00pm Saturday 8th December

Blowers turned the key in the lock and pushed the front door to the mews house on Grosvenor Cottages, Belgravia open. He stepped inside the doorway, dropped his bag and switched on the hallway light.

A flood of memories instantly swept over him. He stood still and took in the sight; everything was just as Faith had left it 2 years ago. Her bike was still standing against the wall in the hallway, her coat hung on the coat stand and her boots were placed neatly beside it. He could hear Faith's laughter coming from the kitchen and he could smell her favourite meal; spaghetti and meatballs, in his nostrils.

Tears started to flow down Blowers face. His heart became heavy and a pain grew in his chest to become unbearable. He picked up his bag, switched off the light, stepped backwards out of the house and slammed the door shut. He took the keys out of the lock and put them into the right-side pocket of his reefer jacket. He turned and walked quickly up the mews to Eaton Terrace where he stopped, dropped the bag and leaned against the wall. Tears were still flowing down his cheeks.

Blowers stood for a couple of minutes in the cold night air staring blankly into the street. He composed himself, took his phone out of his jeans pocket and pressed one on speed dial.

The call was answered on the second ring. "Hello Andrew," the voice on the other end of the line said in a gruff East End accent.

"Hello Tommy. Can I stay in your spare room for a few nights?" Blowers voice quivered.

"Are you okay?"

"I'm fine Tommy. I'm only fifteen minutes away."

Tommy sighed with relief. "Sure, you can stay in the spare room. I'll get out a good bottle of whiskey and we'll catch up on all the news."

"See you in fifteen." Blowers ended the call. He pocketed the phone, picked up his bag and began to walk to his best friend's home.

The walk to Tommy Bowen's antique shop on Witton Place did not clear Blowers head. In his mind's eye, he could see Faith cooking spaghetti and meatballs in the small kitchen in the mews house. Her elegant and perfectly manicured fingers holding an oversized wine glass and taking a sip of her favourite Beaujolais. She flashed her amazing smile, which lit up the room. The wine touched her lips and she stirred the spaghetti sauce. The smell of spaghetti and meatballs drifted through the house.

Blowers snapped out of the dream as his chest began to feel tight again and he started to struggle for breath. He stopped walking and put his right hand up to his chest. Tears began rolling down his face again.

After ten minutes, Blowers had begun to calm down and he resumed his walk to Tommy's shop.

Tommy entered the shop using the stairs from his upstairs apartment. He switched on the lights and saw Blowers through the glass door. As he got closer, he saw his friend sobbing uncontrollably. He quickly opened the door, pulled Blowers through the doorway and gave him a bear hug. "Bloody hell mate, you're a mess."

Tommy held his friend tight for a few minutes and when he had calmed down, he locked the shop door and picked up Blowers' bag. He ushered his friend up the stairs, dumped the bag on the floor next to the rocking chair and began unbuttoning Blowers coat.

Blowers gave him no help at all; he just stood there with silent tears rolling down his face.

Tommy threw his friend's coat over an arm of the sofa and he pushed him to sit down in the rocking chair. He walked over to the drinks cabinet, opened a twelve-year-old bottle of Glenturret single malt whiskey and poured two larges glasses. He took a big mouthful from his glass before walking over to Blowers and putting the glass in his hand.

"Drink it. It'll do you good," he ordered.

Blowers obliged in one mouthful and put the empty glass down on the coffee table in front of him.

Tommy drained his own glass and refilled the two glasses. He took another big mouthful from his glass, leaned back into the sofa and studied his friend.

"Feel any better?"

Blowers did not answer so Tommy raised his voice, "ANDREW!"

Blowers seemed to snap out of the world he had been in and wiped the tears away with the cuff of his jumper.

"What's going on?" Tommy asked with concern. He had never seen his friend like this, not even at Faith's funeral.

"Memories, Tommy. I miss her so much my heart aches."

Tommy felt a deep sadness for his friend's loss. He had lost his soulmate to cancer and he was dying inside. Tommy missed Faith too, but he knew that he had to get Blowers back focusing on the present. "Faith's gone, Andrew. I miss her too but life goes on," he tried to say sympathetically.

Blowers picked up his glass and again downed the whiskey in one mouthful. He looked seriously at his friend. "Sell the mews house for me Tommy."

"Are you sure?"

"Yes," Blowers said firmly.

Tommy downed what was left of his glass of whiskey and again refilled the two glasses. "You're absolutely sure?"

Blowers nodded. "Yes, and you get five percent as an agent's fee."

Tommy raised his glass. "Okay, if that's what you want. Now, tell me what's going on and why you're in such a mess, while we finish this fine bottle of whiskey."

8:00am Sunday 9th December

Blowers was sat at Tommy's breakfast table in yesterday's clothes and had his head in his hands. His head was pounding from the mother of all hangovers. He had forced down a bite of toasted muffin, washed it down with fresh orange juice and instantly felt sick.

It was quiet in the apartment, apart from the rustle of newspaper as Tommy turned a page and the banging in his head. His phone started vibrating on the table; he picked it up and answered softly, "Hello?"

"Ah! Good morning Mr Blowers," said a well-spoken voice on the other end of the call. "It's Henry Potter of Henry Potter Gentleman's Tailor on Saville Row."

Blowers was surprised to get a call from the tailor. "Henry, it's nice to hear from you," he said politely.

"Andrew, how's your hangover?" Tommy said loudly from the other side of the kitchen table.

Blowers gave his friend an icy look. Tommy shrugged and went back to reading the newspaper.

"Just in case you heard that Henry, my hangover is just fine"

The tailor chuckled. "Good-oh!"

"Now, what can I do for you Henry?"

The tailor chuckled again. "Your friend, Mr Bowen, telephoned last night and said you have a client meeting today at Fitch Speciality Insurance, so I've called to tell you that we have four new suits for you to try on. Come to the shop at half past nine this morning and when the fitting is finished, my car will take you to your meeting."

Blowers shot an icy look over at Tommy, who just shrugged and grinned at him.

"I look forward to seeing you at nine thirty, Henry." Blowers ended the call. He turned to Tommy. "You called my tailor while I was passed out in the rocker?"

Tommy put the paper down. "Well you can't go to a meeting at the country's most upmarket insurance company dressed in jeans, an old shirt and a shabby coat, now can you?"

Blowers sighed. "I suppose not."

Tommy stared at Blowers and broke the silence. "Go on then. Chop, chop. Shower and shave. Off you go."

Blowers groaned and got up from the table. His head was still pounding.

Tommy chuckled to himself and went back to reading the newspaper.

9:30am Sunday 9th December

Blowers paid the cab driver with a twenty-pound note and told him to keep the change. He got out of the cab in front of Henry Potter Gentleman's Tailor on Saville Row and shivered as an icy gust of wind blew strongly down the street. He stuffed his gloved hands into the pockets of his Reefer jacket.

The shop door opened and an old man with thinning white hair, a neatly trimmed goatee beard and dressed immaculately in a checked herringbone suit stepped out into the cold morning air. He held his arms wide in greeting. "Mr Blowers. It's been such a long time since we last saw you."

Blowers let the old man hug him. "It's been two years Henry."

The old man released the embrace. "That long, eh. Come in out of the cold and we'll fix you up with four of the finest suits made in London."

Blowers followed the old man into the shop while he continued talking. "Catherine has a pot of tea ready. She's anxious to see you."

"You mean she's anxious to mother me, Henry"

The old man suddenly stopped walking; he turned to Blowers. "Quite so dear boy. How's your hangover?"

Blowers smiled. "It still hurts Henry," and he began looking around the shop, which had an old smell and feel to it.

The old tailor watched him. "Very little has changed since we first opened in Eighteen Hundred and Ten," he proudly announced. The old man continued, "All of the original oak panelling is still on the walls and the light fittings have never been changed from when we first got electricity in Nineteen Twenty Two."

An oak panelled door at the back of the shop opened and a petite old lady holding a fine bone china cup and saucer stepped into the shop. Her white hair was immaculately pinned back in a tight bun on the top of her head, and she was wearing a white, silk blouse and a grey wool, calf length skirt. She announced her presence loudly. "Andrew my dear boy, it's so nice to see you."

Blowers bent down and Catherine Potter gently kissed him on the cheek. She gave him the cup of tea and he took a sip.

"It's nice to see you," Blowers said smiling. He inhaled, "Ah! Chanel Number five."

The old lady winked at him, "A timeless classic."

"Yes, it is," Blowers smiled.

"Catherine! We need to get on. Mr Blowers has an important meeting to attend," Henry Potter barked.

The old seamstress turned, put her hands on her hips and said crossly, "Don't you bark orders at me you old goat."

Blowers smiled to himself. The couple had not changed in the two years he had not seen them. They bickered, but had been married for over 40 years and were still very much in love.

Henry Potter began busying himself with preparing the suits and Catherine nudged Blowers in the ribs. "He still knows who's the boss," she said not too quietly.

"I heard that," the old man said loudly.

"You were meant to my dear." Catherine winked at Blowers.

Blowers took off his coat and hung it on the old coat rack.

Catherine looked Blowers up and down. "You've lost weight, Andrew."

The old tailor turned and also looked Blowers up and down. "Not to worry, we have four suits that will fit you just fine with a little alteration," he said from the back of the shop.

"Don't you need my measurements?" Blowers asked.

The old seamstress grinned, "We already have them. Mr Bowen kindly took them last night."

Blowers just shook his head at the collusion that had gone on between Tommy and the Potters.

The tailor beckoned Blowers to come into the back of the shop for his fittings and Blowers did as he was asked. He began showing Blowers the suits, pointing at each one. "Four suits all of the finest cloth. A black one-button suit jacket with narrow lapels and single vent at the back with a pair of plain front trousers; a grey two-button pin-stripe jacket with a double vent and plain front trousers; a navy-pinstripe double breasted jacket with a double vent and double pleat front trousers and finally, a light grey two-button jacket with narrow lapels and single vent with plain front trousers."

Blowers felt the cloth of each suit. "Very nice Henry," he acknowledged.

The old tailor held up the grey one-button suit. "I suggest we start with this one."

Blowers took the suit from him and went into the changing room. He pulled the heavy, green velvet curtain along the rail and began to change out of his clothes.

Five minutes later Blowers emerged from the changing room wearing the suit. "It feels nice on, Henry," he said admiring himself in the full length, freestanding mirror.

The old tailor studied Blowers for a few seconds and then busily began putting pins in the suit jacket where it needed a slight tuck for a snugger fit and two pins in the trousers for the hem. He then called his wife, "Catherine! We're ready for you to work your magic."

Blowers took this as his cue to change into the next suit. He picked the black one-button suit and went back into the changing room. He took the suit off, and handed it from behind the curtain to the old lady, who went into the back room to make the alterations.

An hour later, Blowers was wearing his new grey two-button, pin-stripe with the double vent. He was also wearing a new blue cotton shirt, a new, dark navy silk tie and a pair of new black oxford shoes. In a new suit carrier, he had the other three suits and in various other bags, he had three new white shirts with double cuffs, a new pair of silver cufflinks, three new silk ties and matching handkerchiefs, six new pairs of black cotton socks, and a pair of new black brogue shoes.

Catherine Potter looked Blowers up and down and remarked, "Very handsome indeed."

"Quite so," her husband chipped in. He continued, "Now, you'll be needing a new top coat for this winter weather and I have just the very coat." He disappeared up the stairs from the shop.

Two minutes later the tailor returned with a long, black, wool coat. "Cashmere wool," he announced. "Feel the quality."

Blowers put the coat on and buttoned it up. He moved his arms up and down. It fit perfectly. He smiled at the tailor. "Everything is perfect as usual Henry."

Catherine handed Blowers a small leather folder containing the invoice for his new clothes. Blowers opened it and raised his eyebrows at the cost.

The old tailor caught the raised eyebrows. "The very best quality and workmanship does not come cheap, Mr Blowers."

Blowers nodded and smiled his acceptance. He knew he was buying the best tailored suits in London. He took his phone out of his inside left jacket pocket, moved his fingers over the touch screen and handed it to the tailor saying, "Just type your account number in and press send, and funds will be transferred directly into your account."

The old tailor did as he was instructed and handed the phone back to Blowers.

"One last thing," Catherine announced and she sprayed a fine cologne into the air.

Blowers picked up his bags and walked through the fine mist.

Catherine grabbed him by the arm and leading him to the door she said, "Now let's get you to your meeting."

Blowers stepped outside into the cold, damp winter air and walked over to a silver vintage Mercedes Benz.

The Driver opened the boot and Blowers put his bags into it. The driver slammed the boot shut. Catherine and Henry Potter had followed Blowers to the car. He shook Henry Potter's hand and gave Catherine a kiss on the cheek.

"Albert will take you to your meeting and then he will take your bags to Mr Bowen's place of residence," the tailor told Blowers.

"Thank you," Blowers said gratefully and got into the rear passenger seat behind the driver. He slammed the door shut.

Henry and Catherine Potter waved goodbye as the car pulled away from the kerbside and then went back into the warmth of the shop. The tailor locked the door, switched off the lights and went upstairs for a cup of tea.

11:00am Sunday 9th December

Blowers got out of the vintage Mercedes Benz and thanked Albert for the ride to Fitch's offices on Leadenhall Street. He watched the car pull away from the kerbside and looked up at the glass building. He sighed. He was back in a world he thought he had left two years ago and he now realised that he was not thrilled about it. He took a deep breath and began to walk up the steps towards the automatic door and into the foyer.

As he entered the building, the Security officer stood up behind the desk. "Mr Blowers?" he said smiling.

"Yes."

"Ah! Good. Mr Fitch is expecting you. Please take the lift to the fifth floor and I'll let Mr Fitch's Personal Assistant know that you're on your way up."

Blowers nodded his thanks and walked over to the lifts. He pressed the up button and stepped into the lift when the doors opened. He pressed the button for the fifth floor and the doors closed.

Blowers stood at the back of the lift and rode up to the fifth floor with his hands dug deep into the pockets of his new top coat. The lift stopped and the doors opened.

"Here goes," he muttered to himself as he stepped out into the carpeted corridor. He stopped abruptly, narrowly avoiding bumping into Fitch's Personal Assistant, who was waiting for him. He apologised, "I'm sorry, Miss."

The Personal Assistant smiled. "Good morning Mr Blowers. It's nice to see you again. If you'll follow me, Mr Fitch is waiting for you in his office."

"It's Jenny, isn't it?"

The Personal Assistant smiled. "Yes. It's nice to be remembered."

Blowers followed the young woman down the corridor to the familiar deep red, mahogany double doors. She stopped at the doors, knocked twice and then pushed them both open. "Please," she indicated with her left hand for Blowers to enter.

Blowers looked at the outstretched left hand. *Still no engagement or wedding ring. A woman who is married to her career as Fitch's Personal Assistant,* Blowers thought to himself as he stepped into an office, which he noticed had not changed since his last visit two and a half years ago.

Fitch was standing behind his antique rosewood desk waiting for Blowers. He extended his right hand for a handshake, which Blowers shook firmly and then indicated with the same hand for Blowers to sit in the high-backed leather chair just to the right of his desk. Blowers unbuttoned his top coat and suit jacket and sank into the comfortable chair.

Still standing, Fitch pushed a photograph of the missing diamond tiara over the desk to Blowers. "Taken when I had the tiara appraised for insurance value, eighteen months ago."

Blowers picked up the photograph, studied it for a minute and put it back down on the desk.

Fitch pushed another photograph over the desk at Blowers. "The tiara was being worn by world renowned urban photographer Robyn Fairbanks, to a charity fundraiser, at the insistence of her mother, the Baroness Cardenham, when she was attacked by an unknown man and relieved of said item."

Blowers picked up the photograph and studied the woman in it. She was beautiful, with a pale complexion, shoulder length fair hair, big brown eyes and a dazzling smile. His heart began to pound in his chest. He put the photograph down on the desk and tried to stay calm.

Fitch smiled. "I'm sure you will agree that she's a beautiful lady."

Blowers nodded. "Yes, she is beautiful."

Fitch continued, "To cut a long story short, the police never caught the assailant. I've had two highly recommended insurance investigators on the case to find the tiara and it is still missing."

Blowers immediately understood why Fitch had tracked him down and visited him personally; he was desperate and he knew that Blowers had resources available to him that the other two investigators did not. He interrupted, "So the waiting period before paying out the full insurance value is twelve months and I'm your last hope for finding the tiara. How long have I got?"

Fitch looked Blowers dead in the eye. "Correct on all counts, Mr Blowers. You've got ten days to find the tiara or I'm five-million pounds poorer and Baroness Cardenham will be that much richer."

"Baroness Cardenham?" Blowers quizzed Fitch. "I've never heard of her."

Fitch let out a short laugh. "I'm not surprised. It's an ancient family line that has been forgotten about and she's been trying for the last two years to restore the family name in high society."

Blowers was puzzled with the connection between the Baroness and Robyn Fairbanks and Fitch saw it, so he continued to explain. "The Baroness married Byron Fairbanks, the American sugar tycoon, in the 1960s, divorced him in the 1980s and had been living in New York high society circles up to two years ago, when she returned to the UK to restore the family name."

Blowers face was deadpan. "Thanks for the history lesson. What makes you think I can find the tiara in ten days when two other insurance investigators couldn't find it in nearly twelve months of looking?"

Fitch smiled. "You have more resources at your disposal than they did."

It was just as Blowers had thought. He got up from the chair and buttoned his jacket and top coat. "If I recover the tiara you'll pay the agreed five percent finder's fee direct into my bank account?"

Correct, just as we have done in the past." Fitch confirmed.

Blowers continued, "And if I don't find it?"

Fitch smiled. "I'll repay all your expenses with an additional twenty thousand pounds for your trouble."

Blowers nodded in agreement and held out his hand, which Fitch shook firmly.

"I'll report to you on nineteenth December, when you'll know whether or not you're paying out to the Baroness."

"Thank you," Fitch said gratefully, "I don't want to be five-million pounds poorer this Christmas."

I bet you don't, Blowers thought to himself and he turned and started walking towards the dark red, mahogany office doors. They opened before he reached them and Fitch's Personal Assistant smiled at him. Blowers smiled back, wished her a good day and walked down the corridor towards the lifts.

The Personal Assistant closed the double doors and as she walked back to her desk, she watched Blowers walk down the corridor. She wondered when she would see the tall, handsome, investigator again.

1:00pm Sunday 9th December

Blowers was sitting in the rocking chair in Tommy's apartment above the antique shop. He had a mug of black tea in his hand and was thinking about how to best use the resources available to him to find the missing tiara in only 10 days. Specifically, he was thinking about how Tommy could help. His friend had friends in lots of places and who no doubt owed him favours. He decided he would need Tommy to use his sources in the Metropolitan Police, so that he could find out how their investigation was now a cold case. He would also need Tommy to reach out to his criminal sources to see what the word on the street was about the theft, and if the thief had made a move to fence the tiara.

Blowers looked up from his mug of tea as Tommy's head appeared on the stairs.

"Good news," Tommy announced, "I've have a buyer for your mews house."

"That was fast."

Tommy sat down on the sofa, leaned back and crossed his right leg over his left. He had a smug look on his face. "It was easy really. Those houses are very much sought after and I have a friend of a friend who's wanted to buy one for a long time." He continued, "He'll pay the full asking price, in cash too"

Blowers took a sip of tea. "And the full asking price is?"

"One-million pounds for a quick sale."

Blowers nodded his agreement and took a sip of tea. "Good. Take care of it please."

Tommy grinned, "It's as good as done mate. I'll go and see my solicitor in the morning to start the paperwork."

Blowers said nothing and took another sip of tea. He would just leave the sale of the house in Tommy's capable hands. He trusted his best friend completely.

A long silence descended on the apartment and Tommy watched the concentration on his friend's face as the time passed by.

He broke the silence, "What's on your mind?"

"The missing Cardenham tiara."

Tommy let out a long low whistle. "It's been missing for nearly a year and they say it's worth about five-million quid. It's a shame that young woman got hurt when it was taken."

Blowers raised an eyebrow. "What else do you know about it?"

Tommy shifted in his seat and began to wish he had said nothing. "Nothing really."

Blowers knew it was an evasive answer and pressed on, "I need you to call in some favours."

Tommy looked at the ceiling. "Oh! Here we go." Blowers ignored his friend's sarcasm. "Please speak to whoever you know at the Met and get me the position on how their investigations are going."

Tommy knew that wasn't all his friend wanted to know. "Okay. And what else?"

"Reach out to your shadier type of friends and let me know what the word on the street is about the theft, and if the thief has tried to fence the tiara."

Tommy shook his head. "That's a lot to ask. But I should tell you that the rumour is that the tiara was out of the county within a week of the theft."

Blowers took a sip of cold tea, pulled a face and put the mug down on the coffee table. He began thinking again.

Tommy got up from the sofa. "I'll make some calls," and he went into his study.

Twenty minutes later Tommy shouted for Blowers to join him in the study. When he walked in, Tommy was sat behind a rosewood writing desk at his laptop and was just ending a telephone call. He pointed to the old two seat sofa, "Have a seat."

Blowers sat. He crossed his right leg over his left and took a sip of cold tea. He had forgotten that it was cold and pulled a face at the taste. He angrily put the mug on the bookshelf to his right.

Tommy started talking, "Baroness Cardenhan throws a fund raising party for her favourite children's charity at the Forbes Gallery. It's one of her calculated plays to establish the family name back into noble society, so anyone with a title and influence is invited. Her daughter, an American and a famous photographer, who's wearing the tiara, goes off alone to look at a Rembrandt and gets attacked. She's punched in the face and relieved of the tiara, a fifty-thousand-pound diamond and ruby necklace and a ten-thousand-pound diamond and ruby ring. None of the items have ever been found and nobody was ever arrested. The daughter goes home to America; the Baroness goes back to wooing noble society and the case goes cold."

Blowers listened intently to his friend and asked, "Who did the police suspect for the assault and robbery?"

Tommy shook his head. "I don't know."

"I don't believe you." Blowers glared at his friend.

Tommy hunched his shoulders and held his hands out. "It's true. I don't know. But my source in the Met's art crime division thought it might be an insurance scam."

The story was now getting interesting. "Carry on," Blowers encouraged.

Tommy sighed. "My source thinks that the tiara, necklace and ring were taken out of the country very quickly by private jet, which accounts for the case going very cold very quickly. The Baroness waits out the twelve-month insurance waiting period and collects the five-million pounds' insurance money. Once the insurance pay-out is made, the thief is informed; the tiara is broken down into individual stones and are sold in a foreign country."

Blowers' mind was now actively working. "Are the police still investigating?"

Tommy shook his head "No. My source says the case is ice cold; one of the coldest they have."

Blowers leaned forward on the sofa. "If it's that cold then it has to be an inside family job."

"How come?" Tommy asked.

"Family stick together and don't talk."

Tommy watched his friend, his face a picture of concentration and after a long minute's silence, Blowers suddenly stood up and said that he needed to go for a walk to think. Tommy watched his friend leave the study and then went back to his laptop.

7:00pm Sunday 9th December

Blowers and Tommy sat opposite each other at a dining table in the Carlingford Gentlemen's club. For an East End boy, Tommy looked like he belonged in the company of Etonians in a private gentleman's club. He was wearing a fine, dark wool suit, a shirt and tie and his shoes were polished to a high military shine. He sat straight backed at the table, a posture he had developed from fifteen years of dinners in the Sergeant's mess.

Blowers looked around the dining room. It was buzzing with conversation in low tones. He had taken the liberty of ordering the food before Tommy arrived. A bottle of red Bordeaux was breathing on the table and a waiter dressed impeccably in white tails put the soup dish down in front of the two men.

Tommy looked at the waiter who smiled and said, "Cream of vegetable. Enjoy."

The waiter poured a little of the wine into Blowers' glass, who tasted it and nodded. He then filled the two glasses, returned the bottle to the table, bowed and then turned and left.

Tommy spooned some soup into his mouth. "Mmmm. Nice," he muttered and put another spoonful into his mouth.

Blowers smiled to himself and put a spoonful of soup in his mouth. It tasted good. He looked over the table at his friend who was enjoying every mouthful. It felt good to see his best friend enjoying himself. He put another spoonful of soup into his mouth and thought, this is going to be a good night.

As Blowers put the last spoonful of soup into his mouth, the waiter who had served them arrived with a trolley containing their main course. He put the empty soup dishes onto the bottom of the trolley and then put plates of roast beef, Yorkshire pudding, roast potatoes and seasonal vegetables down in front of them. He then placed a gravy boat in the middle of the table next to the silver salt and pepper shakers. The waiter bid the two men "Bon appetit," and left the table.

Blowers took a drink of wine and then picked up his knife and fork, cut into the roast beef and put it into his mouth. It was cooked to perfection.

"Lovely," Tommy said, his mouth stuffed with Yorkshire pudding.

The two men quickly demolished the dinner and the waiter again arrived with the trolley and their pudding on it.

Tommy looked at the pudding and exclaimed, "I love spotted dick and custard."

Blowers grinned at his friend.

Tommy tucked straight into the pudding and didn't look up until his dish was empty. He grinned at Blowers. "That was bloody lovely."

"It was, wasn't it," Blowers replied putting the last spoonful of pudding into his mouth.

The waiter reappeared and spoke to the table, "I have taken the liberty of reserving you a table in the snug, where you will find two of our finest Havana cigars, two glasses and a twelve-year-old bottle of your favourite Glenturret single malt whiskey."

Blowers nodded his thanks and deftly slipped a twenty-pound tip into the waiter's hand.

The waiter pocketed the note, bowed slightly in thanks and left the table.

Blowers stood up and said to Tommy, "Bring your glass of wine with you. We'll go and enjoy those cigars and the whiskey."

"Absolutely," Tommy grinned and stood up, pushing his chair backwards.

The two men left the table, walked through the dining room and into the bar. Blowers veered left, opened a heavy wood panelled door and entered the snug. Through a haze of cigar smoke he quickly found the table tucked away in the far-right corner of the room. Just as the waiter had said, there were two cigars and a silver cigar cutter, two glasses and a bottle of Glenturret whiskey on the table.

They sat in the old, cracked, red leather chairs and Tommy drained his glass of wine. He reached for the bottle of whiskey and grinned at his friend.

Blowers smiled back and took a cigar. He clipped the end, lit it and took a long draw in on the cigar.

Tommy poured two large glasses of whiskey and took a large mouthful. He savoured the warmth of the liquid in the back of his throat.

The snug was filled with cigar smoke, the clinking of glasses and the low hum of conversation. Blowers looked through the smoke and around the room, and thought to himself that no doubt deals were being done and plans were being hatched.

Tommy was relaxed and enjoying himself.

Blowers savoured the warmth of the whiskey, as the amber nectar slid down his throat, and the smell of cigar smoke in his nostrils.

"So, tell me what else you've found out?" Blowers suddenly asked his friend.

Tommy was blowing cigar smoke into the air. He reached into his left inside pocket and pulled out a photograph. He gave it to Blowers who studied it and handed it back.

"It's Robyn Fairbanks. She's a beautiful young woman," and he blew smoke into the air. His heart was pounding at seeing a photo of her again.

Tommy nodded. "She's very beautiful and very successful." He continued, "She's the daughter of Baroness Cardenham and Byron Fairbanks. She was assaulted and robbed of the tiara, a necklace and a ring."

Blowers already knew this; he was beginning to become impatient with his friend. "I know all of this Tommy. Did the police suspect her of any involvement in the robbery?"

Tommy shook his head. "No. She was only at the fundraiser as a favour to her father. She's not close to the Baroness and hates everything nobility stands for."

Blowers smiled. "A typical American rebel. Go on."

Tommy took a drink of whiskey and continued. "The Baroness' butler, a man called Boothroyde, I think, heard her arguing on the phone with her father that she didn't want to go to the fundraiser and definitely did not want to wear the tiara."

Blowers sucked deeply on his cigar and blew out smoke. "She's not in on the scam so we can rule her out, and Byron Fairbanks is one of the richest men in the world, so he doesn't need the money. The thief is someone else connected to the Baroness."

Tommy grinned at his friend. "The Butler told the police that five days before the robbery, a nicely dressed and well-spoken man visited Cardenham House and argued with the Baroness."

Blowers' interest now heightened. "What did they argue about?"

"I was just getting to that," Tommy said with a touch of annoyance in his voice.

Blowers apologised for interrupting and Tommy continued his story. "The Butler couldn't hear the argument properly from behind the closed drawing room door, but he told the police that the man was called Thomas Malcom."

Blowers sat up in his chair and leaned forward. "Sir Thomas Malcom?" he said a little too loudly.

Tommy instantly looked around the snug, but it appeared that nobody had heard Blowers. "No. The Baroness' visitor was a young man, not that pompous old prick who keeps telling us at every opportunity he gets on the television that the best thing for Britain is to leave the European Union."

Blowers' mind was now working overtime and asked, "Was Robyn Fairbanks at Cardenham House when Thomas Malcolm visited the Baroness?"

Tommy nodded and blew cigar smoke out into the room. "Yes. Apparently, she caught the butler eavesdropping at the drawing room door."

Blowers downed his whiskey. "Good. I'll start with her. Where is she now?"

Tommy downed his whiskey and then sucked deep on his cigar. "She's showing her latest collection of photographs at the Luciena Gallery in Manchester and on Wednesday, she's selling off her latest collection in a fundraiser at the Luciena Gallery in New York City. All the proceeds are going to a kids' home she supports."

Blowers leaned back in his chair and sucked deeply on his cigar. "Fantastic. A trip to New York it is then. Please get me onto the guest list for Wednesday night. Tell them I'll make a donation of twenty-five thousand dollars to the kids' home on the night."

Tommy stared at his friend.

"What?"

"That's a lot of money, Andrew."

Blowers smiled at his friend. "Yes, it is. You know I was more than financially comfortable before I met Faith and since her death, I have more money than I know what to do with. Faith was always making donations to causes which pulled at her heart strings and since I grew up in the children's home system, I figure that it's time to follow Faith's example."

Tommy raised his glass to his friend, he smiled and took a drink of whiskey. "I'll get it done."

Blowers raised his glass. "Besides, Ms Fairbanks will think I'm a nice guy and hopefully be very cooperative."

After a couple of minutes of silence and enjoyment of the cigars and whiskey, Blowers spoke, "Tommy, see what you can find out about this Thomas Malcolm, will you."

Tommy tipped his imaginary cap. "Yes sir. I'll add it to my shopping list."

Blowers grinned at his friend's sarcasm.

For the remainder of the evening the two friends reminisced, enjoyed their cigars and emptied the bottle of whiskey.

9:30am Monday 10th December

Tommy was downstairs in his shop, so the apartment was empty and Blowers was enjoying some quiet time. He took a bite of toast, picked up the mug of steaming strong black coffee and took a sip. He put the mug back down on the table and picked up his phone. He pressed eight on speed-dial and listened to the phone at the other end ring.

A voice with a hint of a Liverpool accent answered, "Mr Blowers. It's been a while. How can I help you?"

"Yes, it has been a while, John. I'm on a job and I need a flight to New York MacArthur tonight. Are you and your Gulf Stream available?"

The pilot seemed to ignore the question. "It's good to hear from you. How are you keeping? I was so sorry to hear about Faith's passing."

Blowers had not seen the pilot in the two years that had passed since his wife's death, but he could tell from the tone of his voice that he was genuinely sorry. He was determined not to let the sadness of the loss of his wife wash over him. "I get through each day as best I can John. Now, I need a flight to New York tonight; can you help?"

"Of course. The usual fee for you, Mr Blowers. What time do you want to depart?"

"Twenty hundred hours."

"That's fine. I'll file a flight plan with air-traffic-control," the pilot confirmed.

"Great. I'll be on the tarmac at Nineteen Thirty hours. Thanks, John."

"See you then Mr Blowers."

Blowers was just about to end the call when he remembered, "I assume your bank account has not changed, John."

"It's still the same number," the pilot confirmed.

"Good. I'll transfer the money over now." With that, Blowers ended the call and began to transfer the money for the flight into the pilot's bank account.

Blowers picked up the mug of coffee and took another sip. He cradled the mug in his hands and began to make a mental list of the clothes and luggage he would need for his trip. He took another sip of coffee and then scrubbed the list and decided to travel light. He put the mug of coffee down on the table and picked up the phone again. He pressed five on speed dial.

The call was answered on the second ring. "Mr Blowers, it's so nice to hear from you. What can I do for you?"

"Hello Marvin. Are you on a job?"

"Yes sir."

"Can you pick me up at Long Island MacArthur airport tonight at eleven pm New York time? And can I put you on retainer for a few days?"

"Yeah. No problem Mr Blowers."

"The usual fee?"

"Sure. I'll see you at eleven pm tonight." The call ended.

All of Blowers' travel arrangements were now made and he sat back to enjoy the quiet of the apartment and what remained of his breakfast.

Blowers put the last bite of toast into his mouth and swilled it down with the remnants of his coffee. He had decided to take with him his new clothes recently purchased from Henry Potter. He would also need more casual everyday clothes, so he picked up his phone from the table and began to compose an email to Timpson's Gentleman's Outfitters of Manhattan. He ordered two pairs of Levis 501's, six cotton shirts, six white cotton tee-shirts, four lambs wool V-neck jumpers, six pairs of cotton socks, six pairs of silk boxer shorts and one pair of brown leather shoes. The email instructed the shop to deliver his order to his apartment on the corner of Fifth Avenue and East Seventy First Street, Manhattan at ten am on Tuesday eleventh December. The email also asked for the invoice to be sent to his email address. Blowers pressed send and, swapping the phone for the morning newspaper, he sat back in the chair to enjoy his Monday morning.

1:00pm Monday 10th December

Blowers walked down the stairs from the apartment and into Tommy's antique shop. Tommy was charming a middle-aged female customer and Blowers noticed that she was flirting with his friend, with soft delicate touches on his arm and pushing her hair away from her face and behind her ears.

Blowers smiled to himself; his guilty pleasure was watching Tommy charm a sale out of the ladies. He walked slowly and quietly around the shop pretending to be interested in certain pieces of furniture, while all the while he was listening to his friend charm out a sale.

"Look at the quality of this Georgian craftsmanship. Look at the lines, feel the quality of the craftsmanship. Go on, touch it," he heard Tommy say.

The woman ran her fingers along the edge of the writing desk as Tommy was saying, "Imagine the perfect spot in your home, where you can sit with warm, summer sunlight streaming through an open window as you deal with your correspondence."

Tommy had her on the hook and he was reeling her in. Blowers admired his friend's ability as a salesman and thinking back to their days in the parachute regiment, could have ordered him to go into battle un-armed and convince him that he would come out the other end un-harmed. He smiled to himself and shook his head at the thought.

Blowers continued to amble around the shop. He picked up a figurine of a young lady holding a basket of flowers, turned it over in his hands and studied the mark stamped on the bottom.

He heard Tommy say, "Excellent decision, Madam. If you just come over to my desk, I'll complete the paperwork."

Blowers put the figurine down and picked up a silver teapot. He looked over at his friend who was studying a large desk diary.

Tommy looked up at the woman. "If it's convenient, we can deliver the desk to your home at ten o'clock tomorrow morning."

"That will be just fine," the woman said with a smile and pushed some hair away from her face.

Tommy finished writing out the bill of sale and handed it to the woman. He stood and held out his hand for a handshake. "Thank you for your custom."

The woman smiled and lightly shook Tommy's hand. "Thank you," she said softly and picking up her handbag and gloves, she walked towards the door.

Blowers watched the woman leave the shop. He put the silver teapot down, walked over to Tommy's desk and sat down.

Tommy snapped the desk diary shut and grinned at his friend. "That's a nice five-hundred-pound earner."

Blowers complimented his friend, "It's always a pleasure watching you work, Tommy."

"Thanks."

"I've a little job for you to complete by Thursday."

Tommy's face went deadpan. "What is it?"

"Speak to your associates in New York and find a connection between the Baroness and Thomas Malcom."

"The young man who had the argument with the Baroness?" Tommy quizzed.

Blowers nodded. "Yes. I think this is a case of blackmail and I have a feeling it has something to do with when the Baroness first went to New York."

"Information by Thursday?" Tommy said, double checking the request.

"Yes."

"And what will you be doing in the meantime?"

Blowers smiled. "I'm going to New York. I fly out at eight o'clock tonight."

"A private charter flight by any chance?"

Blowers nodded. "Yes. John Thompson's Gulf Stream."

Tommy shook his head.

"Oh! Tommy. Be at Farnborough airport for eight pm on Wednesday. I'll have John fly you over to New York."

"You don't trust email or the telephone?" Tommy teased.

Blowers smiled. "I'd rather hear it from the horse's mouth, and don't you try to kid me that you're not up for a free trip to New York. I'm also sure that you'd like to meet up with Patti."

Tommy shook his head and grinned. "Fuck off." He began to busy himself with some paperwork on his desk.

Blowers let out a short laugh, got up from the desk and walked back up the stairs to the apartment.

7:30pm Monday 10th December

The drive to Farnborough airport was uneventful and Blowers arrived with time to spare. He breezed through airport security with his suit bag and leather holdall and now as promised, he was stood on the tarmac watching Captain John Thompson and his Co-pilot walk down the stairs of the Gulf Stream.

Blowers walked towards the plane and met the pilots half-way. He shook hands with the Captain. "Good to see you again, John. Thanks for being available at such short notice."

"My pleasure, Mr Blowers. It's been a while. You've not met my new Co-pilot, Nick Mollett."

Blowers shook hands with the Co-pilot. "Nice to meet you."

The formalities now over, the group turned and walked to the plane.

Climbing the stairs, the captain updated Blowers on the flight. "We're scheduled with the tower to leave at twenty hundred hours. We'll have a head wind and it'll be a bit bumpy, but we shouldn't lose any more than an hour in time."

Blowers stepped onto the plane and the pilots disappeared into the cockpit. He looked around the cabin; it was spotlessly clean as usual. A locker for his luggage was already open, so he put the suit bag and the holdall in it and slammed the door shut.

He sat down in the soft, leather seat and immediately felt comfortable. He fastened his seatbelt and closed his eyes.

Captain John Thompson emerged from the cockpit and smiled to himself when he saw Blowers asleep.

"Ready?" he asked loudly.

Blowers woke with a start, "What?

"Are you ready for take-off, Mr Blowers?"

"Yes" Blowers said sleepily.

"Good," the pilot grinned. "Let's get cracking then," and he turned and disappeared back into the cockpit, shutting the door behind him.

Blowers closed his eyes again and drifted off·to sleep.

Long Island, New York - 11:30pm Eastern Standard Time - Monday 10th December

In his dreams, Blowers was walking with Faith around the four reservoirs high up on the moors, the Grassholme, Selset, Balderhead and the Hury, just south of Middleton-in-Teesdale. The sun was high in a bright, blue sky and there was a light, warm summer breeze blowing through Faith's long auburn hair. She was holding his hand, their fingers intertwined, and she was telling him in her soft northern Californian accent how peaceful and beautiful it was up on the moors. She suddenly stopped walking and turned to him. She kissed him lightly on the lips and whispered, "I love you". He felt like he was the luckiest man alive. There was a bump and Blowers suddenly woke up. It took him a few seconds to register that he was on a plane and not standing by a reservoir in County Durham, holding Faith's hand. He rubbed his face and focussed his eyes on the cockpit door.

Captain Thompson's voice came over the speaker, "We've arrived safely at Long Island MacArthur airport and only 30 minutes behind schedule."

Blowers rubbed his face again and looked at his watch. It was eleven thirty pm, Eastern Standard Time.

The pilot's voice came over the speaker again, "Prepare to receive US customs officers, Mr Blowers."

The Gulf Stream came to a stop and Blowers unbuckled his seat belt, stood up and stretched. He opened the locker above his head and took out the suit bag and holdall, and put them on the seat next to the one he had been sitting in.

The Co-pilot emerged from the cockpit, nodded to Blowers and opened the plane's door.

Two minutes later, two US customs officers boarded the plane. After checking the flight plan, the plane's paperwork and the two pilots' passports, they turned their attention to Blowers.

"Good evening, Sir. Welcome to the United States of America," the taller of the two officers said with no hint of welcome in his voice.

The shorter officer held out his right hand, "Your passport, please Sir"

As the shorter officer looked through Blowers' passport, his partner asked, "What's the nature of your visit?

"Business. I'm engaged by Fitch Speciality Insurance of London to recover a diamond tiara worth five-million pounds, which was stolen from Baroness Cardenham."

The customs officers looked at each other.

"Really. I am," Blowers smiled.

The shorter customs officer took an ink pad and stamp out of his jacket pocket.

The other officer held his hand up to stop his partner from stamping the passport and asked, "Is that all of your luggage?"

Blowers looked at the luggage on the seat. "Yes. You're welcome to search it."

The shorter of the two officers nodded and his partner stepped over to the suit bag and holdall. He opened the holdall and began to search it.

Five minutes later the search of Blowers' luggage was over and he was thanked for his patience and cooperation. The shorter officer stamped Blowers' passport and handed it to him. Blowers was bid a good evening and the customs officers left the plane.

As the customs officers descended the stairs, Captain John Thompson emerged from the cockpit and enquired, "Everything went smoothly?"

Blowers nodded, "Yes, thanks John."

"Good."

Blowers suddenly remembered, "Oh! John. Can you fly out of Farnborough with my associate, Tommy Bowen, by twenty hundred hours on Wednesday?"

The pilot nodded, "I've got nothing booked in for then, so not a problem."

Blowers nodded his thanks and put his passport into the inside left pocket of his reefer jacket. He slung the suit bag over his left shoulder and picked the holdall up in his right hand. When he got to the plane's open door he turned to the pilot. "Thanks again, and you'll find the fares for mine and Mr Bowen's passage already in your account."

The pilot touched the peak of his cap in thanks.

Blowers descended the stairs from the plane into the freezing, cold night and walked across the tarmac to a waiting Lincoln town car. As he got close, he smiled, transferred the holdall to his left hand and reached out his right hand to shake with the waiting driver.

"It's always good to see you, Marvin"

The big, black man grinned, "Straight back at cha, Mr Blowers."

"How are the Giants doing?" Blowers asked.

"Better than your sorry ass Raiders," the big man quipped back.

Blowers laughed, threw his luggage into the back of the car and followed it inside.

Marvin slammed the door shut and got into the driver's seat. He started the engine, and looked over his shoulder. "To your apartment, Mr Blowers?"

"Yes. Thank you."

The driver turned to face front, he put the car into drive and began to pull off the tarmac towards the airport exit.

Once out on the highway, Marvin started up the conversation, "Are you on vacation, Mr Blowers?"

Blowers shook his head. "No. I'm on a job."

"Just like the old days. You wanna tell?" Marvin grinned into the rear-view mirror.

The driver was good at talking to his customers and Blowers knew that in his business of driving people around New York City, that he picked up bits of information that may be useful to the right person. He also knew that Marvin never gossiped about his customers' business.

"Sure. Why not. Robyn Fairbanks the photographer was assaulted while attending a fundraiser in London organised by her mother, Baroness Cardenham. The thief stole the diamond tiara she was wearing worth five-million pounds, and a ring and a necklace."

Marvin let out a long low whistle. "Wow! That's a lot of dough"

"Yes, it is. I'm chasing the tiara."

A silence descended into the car and Blowers closed his eyes and put his head back onto the headrest. Marvin asked no more questions about the case and when he started the conversation up again, the remainder of the journey to Blowers' apartment was spent talking about football and basketball.

Manhattan, New York City - 10:00am Tuesday 11th December

Blowers sat in the window seat in his apartment drinking a tall glass of freshly squeezed orange juice and eating a toasted bagel, smothered in butter. He was grateful to Mrs Lovric in the apartment down the corridor for getting him some groceries in. He was dressed in sweat pants and a hoody and felt comfortable and relaxed after having had six hours' sleep. That amount of uninterrupted sleep was a rarity these days.

He looked out of the penthouse window across Fifth Avenue and Central Park to the Bethesda Terrace and fountain. He liked being in New York, he felt at home in the city that never sleeps and he smiled to himself as he took another drink of orange juice and watched the world pass by.

His phone buzzed on the seat beside him; he picked it up and answered, "Good morning Tommy. Are you having a good day?"

Tommy was sat at his desk in the shop looking through a sale of contents catalogue for the Sandiford Place auction. "Not bad Andrew. Thanks."

"Have you got me on the guest list to Robyn Fairbanks' exhibition tomorrow night?"

"Yes. You're on the VIP list as a wealthy collector from Durham."

Blowers shook his head. "I'm not from Durham, Tommy. I'm from Taunton in Somerset."

Tommy became irritated at being corrected and said sharply, "You live in Durham so in my book you're from Durham. And don't forget to write a cheque for twenty-five thousand dollars."

Blowers let his friend's sharp tone pass over him and was about to end the call when he remembered, "Oh! Tommy. Don't forget to be on the tarmac at Farnborough airport at seven-thirty pm on Wednesday night."

"I'll be there," Tommy confirmed and the call went dead.

Blowers put the phone down and picked up the glass of orange juice. He gulped it down and finished the glass.

He got up from the window seat and walked across the apartment towards his bedroom, putting the empty glass down on the kitchen counter as he walked by.

Leaving the bedroom door slightly ajar, he went into the bathroom and turned on the shower taps. He stripped out of his sweats, stepped into the steaming shower and closed the glass door. The hot water washed over him from the oversized shower head and quickly steamed up the shower cubical glass.

Faith had often got into the shower with him and he began to imagine that she was with him now. He could feel her hand gently rubbing shower cream into his shoulders and across his chest. Her body was brushing against his as she moved around his body; her skin was so soft. He felt relaxed.

Suddenly she was gone and there was just water pouring over him. His heart became heavy and tears began to roll down his face. He slid down the glass cubical to the tiled floor and pulled his knees up to his chest. He sobbed, his tears mixing with the water, which was pouring down over him.

12:30pm Tuesday 11th December

Blowers walked through the door of the Buoni Amici Café on East Sixty Eighth Street and was shown to a window seat by a young waitress, who had the look of having a bad day written all over her face. Of course, she smiled, was courteous and obliging to the customer's demands but when her back was turned the struggles of the day was there to see.

Blowers had asked for a few minutes to look at the menu and now the waitress was back to take his order. She smiled her strained smile and her note pad and pencil were at the ready to take his order.

He looked up and smiled. "Can I please have the club sandwich with fries and a strong black coffee."

The waitress wrote down his order. "On what bread would you like your club sandwich?"

"White bread, please."

She wrote it down and smiled again. "You Brits are so polite."

Blowers laughed. "Only when we're in a foreign country and want to make a good impression."

The waitress laughed for the first time in the day. She lingered at Blowers' table; she liked the tall, dark haired Brit. His brown eyes had a vulnerability in them and the one-day old stubble enhanced his rugged features.

"Are you on holiday?"

Blowers shook his head. "No. I'm here on business."

"What type of business?"

"I'm an insurance claim investigator."

Blowers didn't want to say anything more, so he politely smiled at the waitress and turned to look out of the window.

The waitress took that as the cue that the conversation was over and walked away to place the order with the kitchen.

Ten minutes later, the waitress brought Blowers' sandwich, fries and coffee to the table.

As she was putting down the coffee, he said to her, "You know, it's only work. Don't let it get you down," and nodding to the outside world through the window, he continued, "Good things happen out there which make you smile and laugh. You just have to pay attention and look for them." He then immediately thought, I should take my own advice.

The waitress was just about to say something when Blowers' phone began to buzz. He smiled his thanks to the waitress and answered the call. "Good afternoon, Marvin."

Marvin was driving through the streets of Greenwich Village and was on speaker. "You'll never guess who I'm on my way to pick up?"

Blowers was not in the mood for games and sighed. "Who?"

"Robyn Fairbanks. She wants taking to the Luciena Gallery on Madison Avenue to make final preparations for her fundraiser tomorrow night."

Blowers was now alert. "Is she a regular customer of yours, Marvin?"

"I've been driving her from time to time for a couple of years now."

Blowers gave Marvin instructions. "Now listen carefully, Marvin. Make polite conversation with her and find out as much as you can about her visit to England a year ago. Try and get her talking about her mother, Baroness Cardenham."

"You got it, Mr Blowers. I gotta go, I'm just pulling up outside of her house now." Marvin ended the call.

Blowers wondered if Marvin would get some useful information out of Ms Fairbanks. He was hopeful but not convinced he could. If she was having a bad day and just didn't want to talk or she thought Marvin was prying into personal matters, Marvin wouldn't get anything useful at all.

Blowers took a bite of the sandwich and settled back in his chair to watch the world pass by on East Sixty Eighth Street.

7:20pm Tuesday 11th December

Since returning to his apartment from lunch at the café, Blowers had spent all of his time on the internet researching Baroness Cardenham from her first arrival in New York in nineteen-sixty-six. He was frustrated because he had found very little information of any use. Although he was intrigued by the fact that she arrived in late January sixty-six and then there was no mention of her in the papers or magazines until Christmas sixty-six, when she exploded onto the New York society scene. There was a black hole of information for 11 months.

Blowers put his phone down on the sofa, leaned back and closed his eyes. He began deep breathing exercises and after a minute began to feel himself becoming less frustrated and more relaxed.

After five minutes, he opened his eyes. He was calm, relaxed and hungry. He decided to go out for dinner and instead of calling Marvin, he decided to take a cab. He grabbed his reefer jacket off the antique hat and coat stand by the apartment door and headed out the door.

London - 2:20pm Tuesday 11th December

Tommy Bowen was sitting at a table tucked away in a discrete corner of the snug at the Carlingford Gentleman's Club. He was waiting for his guest to arrive and he was late. He listened to the low hum of conversation and guessed that secrets were being told, deals were being made and plans were being made. He took a large mouthful of whiskey and then sucked deeply on the Cuban cigar. He blew smoke out into the air and checked his watch again. As he looked up, he saw his guest being shown through the snug's door by the Head Butler.

He rose from his seat and held out his right hand to greet his guest, "Lord Watson. Thank you for agreeing to meet me."

The peer shook Tommy's hand firmly and sat in the soft, red, leather chair opposite. Tommy sat down and the Head Butler offered to pour the peer a glass of whiskey.

"Twelve-year-old Glenturret, Crieff's finest export," Tommy informed the peer.

The peer nodded to the Head Butler who poured him a large glass full.

"Would his lordship like a cigar?" the Head Butler enquired.

"Please."

The Head Butler clipped the end of the cigar, handed it to the peer and then lit the end.

The peer sucked deeply on the cigar and blew smoke out into the room.

The Head Butler then nodded to the table, turned and left the snug.

The peer took another deep suck on the cigar and smiled at Tommy. "Smoother than the inside of a debutante's thighs, but not quite as risky."

Tommy laughed.

"It's nice to see you again, Mr Bowen. Now, what do I owe the pleasure?"

Tommy pushed a photograph across the table.

"It's a rosewood writing desk from the time of the American War of Independence. It's just arrived from Philadelphia and I thought I would give you first look at it."

The peer smiled at Tommy and pushed the photograph back across the table. "Now, now, Mr Bowen. We're meeting in a very private corner of a gentleman's club; this conversation is not about a writing desk. You could have easily telephoned the house and invited me to your shop to look at the desk."

Tommy shifted in his chair and lowered his voice, "I'm helping out a friend and I was hoping that you might be able to give me some information about someone."

The peer considered Tommy's words for a moment. "Mmmmm. And who might that someone be?"

Tommy still kept his voice low, "Baroness Cardenham."

A serious look appeared on the peer's face.

"What about her?" he said a little too sharply.

Tommy took a drink of whiskey. "I was wondering if you could tell me anything about why she went to New York in nineteen-sixty-six."

The peer thought for a minute and took a drink of whisky. He crossed his left leg over his right and swilled the whiskey around in his glass. "Is this to do with the theft of the tiara?"

Tommy was beginning to feel uncomfortable and he shifted in his chair. "Maybe."

The peer saw Tommy's discomfort and decided he was enjoying himself. He took another large mouthful of whiskey and decided he would tell Tommy what he knew. "Well, I don't like the woman. Never have. The Cardenhams spent Christmas in nineteen-sixty-five with Sir Thomas Malcom and stayed on for New Year. Sir Thomas was well known for having 'a thing' for young ladies and the rumour back then was that he and young lady Cardenham had a short passionate affair."

Tommy was listening intently and blew cigar smoke into the air. "So why does she go to New York?"

The peer let out a short laugh. "My dear boy, she was packed off by her father, the Baron, to avoid a scandal."

Tommy though for a moment. "She was pregnant?"

The peer took another suck on his cigar. "According to the rumours."

Tommy nodded and the peer looked at his watch. "Mr Bowen, I have an appointment at half past three and must now leave you. Thank you for the cigar and whiskey. And of course, this conversation never took place."

Tommy stood and shook the peer's hand and as he turned to leave the table, Tommy spoke, "Oh! Lord Watson. I shall have the rosewood writing desk delivered to your house tonight. A gift. Do as you please with it."

The peer smiled, tipped his imaginary hat in thanks and left the snug.

Tommy sat back down in his chair and poured himself another large glass of whiskey. He took a large mouthful, sucked deeply on the cigar and smiled to himself. The information from Lord Watson was worth the trade for the antique rosewood writing desk.

Manhattan, New York City -7:30pm Tuesday 11th December

On his way through the lobby of his apartment building, Blowers stopped to talk to the concierge, "Hi Marty. Can you recommend a good Italian restaurant?"

The concierge thought for a few seconds and shook his head. "No. Sorry Mr Blowers, not close by."

Blowers thanked the concierge and started walking towards the door, but before he reached it, the concierge called out, "Mr Blowers. I've heard that the Ariana on Perry Street between Hudson and Greenwich in Greenwich Village is very nice."

"Thanks, Marty," Blowers shouted without looking back.

Blowers stepped out of the apartment building and into the freezing night air. He stood on the sidewalk, looking up and down Fifth Avenue for a cab. A strong, cold wind was blowing from the North East down the street and he wished he had brought his Harris Tweed cap out with him. He pulled the collar of his reefer jacket up around his ears, hunched his shoulders against the cold and pushed his gloved hands deep into his coat pockets.

After a couple of minutes of walking on the spot to keep warm, he saw a cab heading his way. He stepped towards the kerb, raised his right arm and hailed it. The cab pulled over and he got in.

"Where to buddy?" the driver asked loudly.

"To the Ariana on Perry Street between Hudson and Greenwich in the village."

"You got it," the driver said happily and the cab pulled away from the kerbside into the evening traffic.

Thirty minutes later, the cab pulled up outside of the Ariana and Blowers paid the driver with a fifty-dollar bill. He told him to keep the change and the driver touched the peak of his Yankees baseball cap.

"Thanks buddy. Have a nice night," the driver said happily and then drove the cab into the night's traffic.

Blowers' phone buzzed in his inside left coat pocket. He dug it out and saw that it was Tommy calling.

"Hello Tommy."

"The rumour is that she was shipped off to New York in January sixty-six because she was pregnant."

Blowers pulled the collar of his coat up around his ears with his free hand.

"A reliable source, Tommy?"

"Very reliable. Lord Watson."

"Well that makes sense." Blowers said to himself but down the phone.

"What makes sense?" Tommy asked.

"Oh, nothing Tommy. It's just a little puzzle I've been wrestling with all day. What did this information cost you?"

"A rosewood writing desk from the American War of Independence period. I had it shipped over from Philadelphia."

"I owe you one Tommy."

"Andrew!"

"What?"

"You owe me a lot for all the favours I've done for you over the years."

Blowers laughed but he knew his best friend was right and after saying, "Thanks," he ended the call.

Blowers put the phone back into his coat pocket, turned, and walked to the restaurant door. As he opened the door, a young woman who was waving her goodbyes to some friends and was trying to have a conversation on her phone at the same time, bumped into him. Her bag slipped off her shoulder, the folder she was carrying went sprawling across the wet floor and she nearly dropped the phone. She bent down immediately to pick up the folder.

As she rose, Blowers noticed that she was blushing in embarrassment. He quickly decided to apologise first, "I'm so sorry Miss. It was all my fault. I should have been more careful."

Still looking down, the young woman shook her head. "No. No. It was my fault. I should have been looking where I was walking." She raised her head and gave an embarrassed smile.

Blowers immediately recognized that the young woman was Robyn Fairbank. She had the most gorgeous big brown eyes and was more beautiful in person than the photograph had shown. Before he could say anything else to her, she pushed past him and walked towards a waiting cab. He turned and watched her walk to the sidewalk and the waiting cab.

She was wearing black leather boots with a two inch heel, skin tight jeans tucked into the boots and a dark brown leather coat with a belt tied around her slender waist. Her fair hair was blowing in the cold, winter wind. His heart was pounding and he thought it was going to burst out of his chest. He watched the cab pull away from the kerbside.

As the cab pulled away from outside of the restaurant, Robyn Fairbanks looked out of the window at the man she had just bumped into. He was tall and looked to have an athletic build under the thick, black, woollen coat. When she had first looked up at him she had noticed that his dark brown hair was cut short and was turning grey at the temples. The stubble on his face gave his chin a rugged look and his dark brown eyes had sadness in them. The lines on his face betrayed that he had seen a lot of life. He was very handsome and her heart was racing. She sighed and leaned back into the cab's back seat.

The driver looked in the rear-view mirror at the beautiful young woman slouched in the back of his cab and looking out of the window. "Are you ok miss?"

"Yes. I'm fine. Thanks."

Still looking in the rear-view mirror, the cab driver asked, "Where to?"

She suddenly snapped out of her daydream. "What?"

"I asked where do you want to go, lady?"

She blushed. "Oh! Sorry! Washington Square North between Macdougal and Fifth Avenue."

"Okay," the cab driver acknowledged.

As Robyn rode home in the cab, she looked out of the window and thought about the man she had bumped into. She had never felt like this before; her heart was still racing and it felt like the blood was rushing through her veins. She realized that she was sweating, so she reached into her purse and pulled out a Kleenex. She dabbed at her forehead and took a deep breath. She could not get the picture of the handsome stranger out of her head.

When the cab was out of sight, Blowers opened the door to the restaurant and entered. He looked around the busy restaurant and didn't register the waitress saying, "A table for one, Sir?" His heart was racing and he could still see Robyn Fairbanks' big brown eyes looking up at him.

He suddenly returned to the present when the waitress raised her voice, "SIR!"

"Oh! Sorry Miss. A table for one please."

The waitress smiled and indicating with her right hand said, "This way."

On the short walk to his table, Blowers realised that because of the incident tonight with Ms Fairbanks, his meeting her tomorrow night at the fundraiser could be quite awkward. The situation was an inconvenience and a problem he would have to solve.

2:00am Wednesday 12th December

When Blowers had gotten back to his apartment, he headed for the drinks cabinet. He poured himself a large glass of Glenturret whiskey and downed it in one. Then he poured himself another and took the bottle with him into his bedroom. He drank, finished the bottle and passed out on the bed.

Blowers sleep had been fitful. Since he had bumped into Robyn Fairbanks at the restaurant, he had not been feeling his normal self. He could not get the image of her beautiful face and slim body out of his head. He had picked at his food and the waitress had asked him more than once if his food was okay. He had smiled and said, "Yes, thank you," and the waitress had smiled back, but he knew that she had not believed him.

Now he was wide awake. He rubbed his face and stretched. He got up off the bed and walked through the darkness to the kitchen. He switched on the light, took a tall glass from the shelf, opened the refrigerator and took out a carton of milk. It smelled okay, so he filled the glass. Then after taking two chocolate chip cookies out of the glass jar on the counter, he walked over to the window seat and looked out over Fifth Avenue and Central Park. He took a bite of one of the cookies and swilled it down with a large mouthful of cold milk.

He began to daydream. His mind wandered back to Christmas Eve 2001 in Franco's Bar in San Francisco. He was supposed to be at the opera with a client, but instead he was enjoying a double Speyside single malt whiskey at the bar. Music was playing and the place was hot and loud. People were out with friends, family and work colleagues enjoying the start of the holidays. He was talking to the bar tender about the Forty Niners season so far, when he heard a commotion coming from the entrance to the bar. He turned to see what was happening. The most beautiful woman he had ever seen, was surrounded by people and she was signing autographs. He could not take his eyes off the woman; her auburn hair was immaculately styled and around her neck, she wore a pearl necklace. The black evening gown accentuated her slender figure and he estimated that without the three-inch heels, she was at least five foot seven inches tall. He watched her struggle through the crowd and eventually she arrived in the spot next him at the bar. She ordered a bourbon straight up. Blowers smiled, as he remembered the conversation that followed.

"Dreadful stuff," he had said to himself.

She turned to him. "Excuse me!"

He had looked up and saw that she was staring at him. He then nodded towards the room and said, "You're popular."

"I guess I am," she had answered back.

He had smiled at her answer and turned back to his drink.

He then turned back to the woman when he thought he heard her say, "The price of being famous."

"You're famous?"

She glared at him. "Seriously? You're kidding, right?"

He didn't have a clue who she was. "No, I'm not kidding. Are you famous?"

She had then begun to laugh and after about a minute she said, "You must be the only person in this place who doesn't know who I am." She held out her hand, "I'm Faith Roberts."

Blowers remembered how soft her long slender fingers had felt in his hand and he smiled to himself. He told her his name and then offered to replace her bourbon with a proper glass of whiskey. She refused, saying that she would rather stick with the dreadful stuff from Clermont, Kentucky. He had acknowledged her loyalty by raising his glass.

Blowers smiled at the memory, stuffed what remained of the cookie into his mouth and washed it down with another mouthful of milk.

He again thought back to his first meeting with Faith. They had talked and drank until two am and not once did they talk about their jobs. They talked about the music and films they liked, the places in the world they had been to and the different types of food they liked. It was the most perfect night, which ended with Faith giving him her number and them arranging a dinner date for three days' time. She had made his heart race and waiting three days to see her again was torture.

Blowers downed the milk and put the empty glass onto the plate next to the uneaten cookie.

"Fuck," he said quietly to himself. He had just realised that he was experiencing the same feelings for Robyn Fairbanks as he did when he first met Faith.

He sat in the window seat looking out over Fifth Avenue, trying to work out what to do about his feelings and how they would affect the job of recovering the tiara.

By the time the sun began to rise, Blowers had still not solved the problem. He got up from the window seat and walked to his bedroom for a shower. Maybe the answer would come to him as he let the water wash over him, but he did not hold out much hope of that.

10:30am Wednesday 12th December

The bell on the door of Pisconti Gentleman's Barbers on East Forty First Street in Midtown rang, as Blowers walked through the door. A voice shouted from the far end of the shop. "Hey! Andy Blowers. What you doing here man?"

Blowers raised his right hand and half waved.

The barber excused himself from his customer, walked over to Blowers and hugged him.

"I came for the best haircut and shave in Manhattan from Gino Pisconti."

The barber stepped back, looked Blowers up and down and smiled. "You've lost weight man."

Blowers patted his stomach, "Just a little bit."

The barber laughed and said, "You only come in here when you've got something going on man. You got a date?"

Blowers shook his head. "No. A fundraiser at the Luciena Gallery on Madison Avenue tonight."

"That's the Robyn Fairbanks exhibition. Right?"

Blowers smiled. "Yes, it is," and looking around the shop full of customers he asked, "Can you fit me in for a haircut and shave?"

The barber slapped Blowers on the shoulder and grinned. "Sure. For you, anytime," he said loudly. "Take a seat pal. I'll finish up with Mr Keane and then you're next. Marco and Franco can take care of the other customers."

Blowers unbuttoned his reefer jacket and hung it on the peg on the wall. He sat down on the old faded velour seat and the barber went back to his customer to finish his haircut.

Blowers thumbed through the magazines on the table and settled for an American muscle car magazine. He got himself comfortable and began to read the article on page two about the nineteen-sixty-four Pontiac GTO.

Twenty minutes later, Blowers was sat in the barber's chair having his hair cut. He looked at the barber through the large mirror on the wall. "Gino, this place hasn't changed in the ten years I've been coming here."

The barber stopped cutting. "Man. This place hasn't changed since twenty-nine when my grandpop opened the shop."

Blowers smiled at the barber through the mirror. "It has character. I like it."

The barber looked around the shop. "It has plenty of that man," and he continued to snip away at Blowers' hair.

The barber updated Blowers about what had happened in the shop and in his family in the two years he had been away, and said he was sorry to hear about Faith's death. Blowers thanked him for his kind words and his eyes began to well up with tears. The barber stopped cutting and handed Blowers a Kleenex.

Blowers wiped his eyes and told the barber about how for two years he had been hiding out on a farm in the North East of England, and about the new car business he had set up with Davy.

"You're not selling cars here are you man?" the barber enquired.

Blowers laughed. "No. I'm here chasing down stolen jewels for an insurance company in London."

The barber paused his cutting. "Stepping back in time. Just like the old days," he said smiling at Blowers through the mirror.

Blowers looked back at the barber. "I guess so. This will be one of the few cases I will do. I'm going to pick and choose them to suit me. I don't want to get back into this life full time. I'm excited about the new car business."

"Whatever makes you happy man," and the barber went back to snipping away at Blowers' hair.

Forty-five minutes after getting into the chair for a haircut and shave, Gino Pisconti announced that he was finished.

Blowers looked in the mirror and liked what he saw. "I mean it. The best damn haircut and shave in Manhattan."

The barber bowed and Blowers got up out of the chair. He reached into his jeans pocket, pulled out his wallet and opened it. He gave the barber a one-hundred-dollar bill and told him to keep the change.

The barber bowed again. "Man, you're generous."

Blowers smiled. "Consider the tip as payments for all the haircuts I've missed in the last two years."

"I will. Thanks man," and the barber put the money into the till.

Blowers retrieved his coat from the peg on the wall and put it on.

The barber hugged Blowers and patted him on the back. "It's always nice to see you man. Don't leave it so long between visits."

"I won't," Blowers promised. He buttoned his coat, waved goodbye and stepped out of the shop into the cold, winter day.

7:30pm Wednesday 12th December

Blowers had been in the shower for twenty minutes, just letting the hot water wash over his body. The warmth had seeped into his very being and he was totally relaxed. He felt like his soul had been cleansed.

His phone began to ring and he turned off the shower. He opened the door, stepped out on to the heated stone tiles and grabbed the phone off the shelf. "Hello Marvin. How are you?"

"I'm fine man. I'm just letting you know that I'm ten minutes out. I'll be parked out front."

"Okay, Thanks." Blowers ended the call.

Blowers cursed himself, he had been in the shower too long. He needed to get a move on and now it would be a rush to get dressed and to the fundraiser on time for its start. He grabbed the large, fluffy white towel from the heated rail and began to quickly rub himself dry.

When he was finished, he left the towel on the bathroom floor and walked naked into his bedroom.

He looked at the clothes he had selected for the evening and was satisfied with his choice. He quickly put on some dark blue, silk boxers, a pair of grey, cotton socks and a white double cuff shirt. He then put on the grey pinstripe trousers and buckled the black leather belt. After fastening the laces of his new black oxford shoes, he turned his attention to choosing a tie.

He chose the dark navy silk tie over the black and grey ones and tied it with a Windsor knot. He grabbed the suit jacket off the hanger, put it on and fastened the top button.

He inspected himself in the full-length mirror, adjusted the shirt cuffs and smiled. He liked what he saw. He then turned and grabbed the new top coat off the hanger and put it on as he rushed through the apartment and out of the door.

After telling the concierge that he was expecting his friend, Tommy Bowen, to arrive tonight and instructing him to give him the spare key, Blowers stepped out of the apartment building and into the cold night.

He took the few steps to the waiting Lincoln town car with its engine running, opened the rear passenger door and got in.

"Sorry I kept you waiting Marvin."

Marvin looked at Blowers in the rear-view mirror. "No problem, Mr Blowers. To the Luciena on Madison, right?"

"Yes please."

Marvin put the car into drive and pulled away from the kerbside.

On the short trip to the gallery, Blowers asked Marvin what he'd found out from Robyn Fairbanks about her trip to England.

Marvin shrugged and talked to him through the rear-view mirror. "Nothing man. She said she didn't like London much and was happy to be home in New York City."

Blowers had suspected that Marvin wouldn't have found out anything useful, but it had been worth the try.

8:05pm Wednesday 12th December

Blowers walked through the doors of the Luciena Gallery, gave his name to the concierge who checked it off the VIP list and then handed his coat to one of the cloak room attendants, who gave him a ticket with a number on it.

He pocketed the ticket.

The concierge smiled. "Welcome, Mr Blowers. Please take a glass of wine and have a good evening."

Blowers nodded his thanks, took a glass of red wine and surveyed the room. He didn't see anyone he knew. He then looked for Robyn Fairbanks but couldn't see her, so he moved to his left to look at some of the photos on show.

He had been making his way around the exhibits for fifteen minutes when Robyn Fairbanks arrived. He was looking at a black and white photo of some young men playing basketball in a city playground, when the sound of applause made him turn around. He saw a beautiful young woman wearing a long, grey, silk, evening gown which accentuated her slender figure. His heart began to pound and he began to sweat. He pulled a white cotton handkerchief out of his trouser pocket and dabbed at his forehead. He needed to calm down, so he turned his attention back to the photo.

Five minutes later, Blowers was still looking at the photo of the basketball players. It captivated him, he could see their passion, energy, movement and sweat.

"You like that one, huh!"

Blowers heard the voice over his left shoulder. He turned. "Yes. I do."

Robyn Fairbanks was startled. "You!"

"Yes. Me." Blowers smiled and held out his right hand in greeting, "Andrew Blowers."

She took his hand and lightly shook it. Her heart was beating fast and she was trying her best to keep calm.

"I'm Robyn Fairbanks and I'm pleased to meet you, Mr Blowers."

Blowers gave a little nod, "Likewise."

They stood holding hands and in silence for a couple of seconds and then realising that her hand had lingered too long in his, she slowly withdrew her hand. She thought quickly of something to say to take away the awkwardness. "Are you a collector?"

Blowers shook his head. "No."

"Are you a critic?"

He shook his head again.

Robyn laughed nervously. "Are you a stalker?"

He shook his head a third time. "No. Not one of those either."

She was puzzled. "So, what are you?"

Blowers decided that the truth from the outset was the best policy, even though he knew that her reaction would not be a good one. He looked her dead in the eyes and said as softly as he could, "I'm an insurance investigator."

Robyn felt anger immediately build up inside her. "You son of a bitch! You bastard! This is about that fucking tiara, isn't it," she hissed as quietly as possible. She turned to walk away from Blowers and then turned back and said a bit too loudly, "So you bumping into me the other night at the restaurant was a set up?"

Blowers put his hands in his pockets and looked around room; some of the other guests were now staring at them. He knew he was on thin ice and needed to calm the situation immediately, if he was going to get Robyn's help on the case. He shook his head and his eyes were pleading, "No. It's not how it looks. The other night wasn't a set up. It was a total coincidence."

Robyn just stood staring at him. She couldn't decide whether or not to believe him and Blowers could see it in her face.

"I came tonight to see if your photography is as good as people have been saying and to give you this." He reached into his inside, left, jacket pocket and pulled out a cheque and handed it to her. "Please take it. It's for twenty-five thousand dollars. You just need to fill in the kids' home name on the payee line."

Robyn just stared at Blowers. She was even more confused now.

Blowers explained, "I grew up in Local Authority care back in England, so I know what it's like for the kids. Please take it," he pleaded.

Robyn snatched the cheque out of his hand. "Thank you. It's very generous," and she put it in her tiny clutch bag.

Blowers inwardly let out a sigh of relief.

Robyn turned and walked away. She took a glass of white wine from a waitress, downed it in one mouthful, smiled to herself and began talking to a tanned, grey haired man and his wife.

Blowers decided that the best policy for now was to mind his own business, so he continued to move around the exhibition, spending a good length of time at each photograph and trying to get a feel for each one.

On two occasions, his eyes met Robyn's and each time she gave him a slight smile. He smiled back and his heart beat faster. He felt like he was engaged in an emotional dance with her. He was nervous, a feeling he had not felt since his first proper date with Faith.

As the evening began to come to an end and guests began to leave in their chauffeur driven limousines, Blowers went back to the photograph of the basketball players.

He felt a presence at his shoulder. "I really do like this one," he said without looking to see who was standing behind him.

"It was the photograph that launched my career," a soft voice replied.

He turned around and smiled at Robyn. "How much is it for sale for?"

Robyn shook her head. "Oh! It's not for sale. I show it at every exhibition. I'm very attached to it"

"I really am pleased to donate to the kids' home," Blowers said sincerely.

Robyn smiled. "Thank you," and she lightly touched his arm. She then turned and sat down on one of the gallery benches.

Blowers followed, sat down beside her and asked, "How much did you raise tonight?"

"Oh! About one-hundred and fifty-thousand I think." She looked him in the eyes and said, "I'm not sure what I can tell you about the theft of the tiara. I told the cops everything I know and I'm sure you've read my statement and seen the security video tape."

Blowers thought for a moment. "Is there anything you might not have told the police, like a certain smell or..."

She cut him off, "His cologne."

Blowers' radar was now fully switched on. "What about his cologne?"

"It was the same as a man called Thomas Malcolm was wearing when he visited the Baroness."

Blowers nodded. "Okay. Tell me about the visit."

Robyn began the story. "I saw and heard him introduce himself to the Baroness as Thomas Malcolm from New York City. When the Baroness heard this, the colour drained away from her face. It was like she'd seen a ghost. She quickly ushered him into the library and locked the door. I thought nothing of it until I caught the Butler listening at the door. I was feeling kinda nosey so I threatened him with telling the Baroness that he was eavesdropping, if he didn't tell me what was going on. He told me that he'd heard the man tell the Baroness that he was her son and that there would be a scandal if it got out. The Butler said that he demanded five-million pounds to keep the secret."

Blowers listened intently to the story, never breaking eye contact with Robyn while she told it.

"How can you be sure about the smell of cologne?"

Robyn smiled. "I answered the door and I got a good whiff of it as he walked past me into the lobby."

Blowers thought for a moment. "That's very helpful Ms Fairbanks." He now had all the pieces in the puzzle.

There were a few seconds of silence between them and then he decided to be brave. "I'm very grateful for your time Ms Fairbanks and as a thank you, I'd like to cook you dinner."

Robyn felt her heart starting to race even faster and could not stop herself from saying, "Yes. I'd like that."

Blowers smiled. Robyn held out her hand and said, "Please call me Robyn."

He took her hand and grinned stupidly. His heart rate was also increasing and he was relieved at not being turned down. "Are you free tomorrow night?"

"Yes."

"Good. I have an apartment on Fifth Avenue." He gave her his card with his cell phone number on it. He continued, "Text me your address and I'll send a car to pick you up at seven thirty."

Robyn took the card and Blowers stood up. He took a few steps towards the cloak room to collect his coat and then turned back to Robyn. "By the way, you look very elegant in Chanel."

She smiled, "Thank you."

Blowers retrieved his coat from the cloak room, and stepped out into the freezing, winter night. He decided that he would walk back to the apartment, so he pulled up the collar of his top coat and pushed his hands deep into its pockets. He began walking and there was a slight spring in his step.

Robyn looked at the card and took her phone out of her clutch bag. She texted her address to the number on the card.

"Is everything okay Ms Fairbanks," a voice said from behind her.

Robyn stood up and faced the gallery curator. "Yes. Thanks. Please have my car drive around to the front of the gallery."

The curator nodded. "Certainly," and he walked away.

Blowers' phone buzzed in his coat pocket. He took it out and smiled at the address on the screen. His heart rate increased some more.

12:30am Thursday 13th December

Blowers walked through the lobby of his apartment building, whistling the tune to 'What a wonderful world.' He was happy.

"A good night Mr Blowers?" the concierge asked.

"Yes. Thanks," he replied, while continuing to walk past the concierge desk.

"Mr Blowers," the concierge shouted after him.

Blowers stopped and turned "Yes?"

"Your guest has arrived. I gave him your spare key and sent him up to your apartment as instructed."

"Thank you," Blowers said with a smile and walked to the elevators while continuing to whistle 'What a wonderful world.'

Blowers walked into his apartment to find Tommy reading an antiques magazine and helping himself to what was left of a bottle of twelve-year-old Glenturret whiskey.

"Making yourself at home I see," he said grinning at his friend.

Tommy raised his glass in reply and took a big mouthful of the golden liquor.

Blowers took off his coat and hung it up on the antique coat stand. He then sat on the sofa and got right down to business. "Robyn Fairbanks has told me that Thomas Malcolm told the Baroness that he is her son and that he wanted five-million-pounds to keep quiet."

Tommy took a drink of whiskey and thought for a moment. "That ties in with what Lord Watson told me. He said that there was a rumour back in nineteen sixty-six that the Baroness was pregnant by Sir Thomas Malcolm, and that she was packed off to New York to have the baby and avoid a scandal."

Blowers got up from the sofa and got himself a glass from the drinks cabinet.

Tommy poured him a large whiskey and then topped up his own glass.

Blowers took a drink. "I did some searching on the internet. The Baroness arrived in New York in late January sixty-six and then there was no mention of her in the papers or magazines until Christmas sixty-six, when she announced her presence on the New York society scene. There is a black hole of information for 11 months."

Tommy wagged his finger and picked up on Blowers thoughts. "She had the baby and when it went for adoption, she was free to party."

Blowers took a large mouthful of whiskey. "My thoughts exactly."

"So, you need to check adoption records Andrew."

Blowers shook his head. "No. I'm guessing that the Cardenhams didn't want anyone to know about the baby, so it was adopted privately. I doubt there was any paperwork at all."

There was a long minute's silence and then Blowers spoke. "Robyn said that Thomas Malcolm had a New York accent. My guess is that he found out who his biological father is, took his name and then found out who his mother is. I'm betting that the Baroness has a cash flow problem and the blackmail presented her with the opportunity to commit insurance fraud, with Thomas Malcom's help. The tiara is never found because it's here in New York City, the insurance is paid out and hey presto, the Baroness has five million pounds to play with."

Tommy drained his glass. "So the Baroness cooked up a plan for Malcom to steal the tiara and he can do what he likes with the diamonds, so long as he keeps his mouth shut. And the Baroness collects the insurance pay out. That's two problems solved in one fell swoop."

Blowers raised his glass to acknowledge his friend's deduction and said, "I think that Malcolm got the diamonds out of the UK within twenty-four hours and brought them here to where he feels safe, New York City."

"Do you think Robyn Fairbanks was in on the plan?" Tommy asked.

Blowers shook his head. "No. I don't. And that reminds me, she's coming over for dinner tonight."

Tommy began coughing, "What!"

Blowers pointed at his friend. "You be on your best behaviour."

Tommy grinned mischievously. "Oh! I will."

Blowers looked at his watch and suddenly got up from the sofa. "Right. Time for bed I think," and he drained his glass. The warmth of the liquor felt good in the back of his throat.

Tommy agreed and stood up.

Blowers patted his friend on the shoulder. "Have you made yourself comfortable in the spare bedroom?"

"Yes, very comfortable. Thanks."

"Good."

Blowers went into his bedroom and closed the door behind him. He loosened his tie and took his phone out of his left inside jacket pocket. He pressed four on speed dial for Fitch, who answered on the second ring.

"Mr Blowers. What news have you got for me?"

Blowers told Fitch everything he had found out and his theory about the Baroness being blackmailed and committing insurance fraud with Thomas Malcom's help.

"So how do you plan to track down this Thomas Malcom?" Fitch asked.

"I have a friend who works for the FBI's white collar crime division here in New York and I think he will help. He owes me a favour or two."

It was music to Fitch's ears and he said, "Okay. Good."

"But Mr Fitch, it might take some time to track Thomas Malcom down, so there's a possibility that I won't meet the deadline of the nineteenth," Blowers warned.

There was silence on the other end of the call.

"Mr Fitch?"

Fitch spoke. "Okay. If you haven't recovered the tiara by the nineteenth, I'll stall on the pay out. But do everything you can to find it." The call then went dead.

Blowers sat on the bed and let out a slow exhale of breath. He put the phone on the nightstand and undressed. He put on a pair of cotton pyjama bottoms, switched off the lamp and got into bed. He closed his eyes and wondered how long it would take for the nightmares to come.

04:00am Thursday 13th December

Blowers' face was screwed up tight, his head was tossing from side to side and his arms and legs were thrashing about.

He was back on Mount Longdon in the Falkland Islands on eleventh June nineteen-eighty-two. The darkness closed in all around him and the freezing cold of the South Atlantic winter chilled him to the bone. All around him there were flashes and bangs of grenades and mortars exploding. The night air was thick with bullets from heavy machine guns, rifles and semi-automatic weapons, which were ricocheting off the rocks and biting home on both sides. He could hear orders being shouted and the screams and sobbing from the men on both sides who lay wounded and dying. Somewhere close by, a comrade was calling for his mother. He heard a thud as a bullet struck home in the man crouching next to him behind the large boulder. He was alone now, where was his platoon? He looked around, it didn't matter, he had to keep moving forward. If he wanted to live he had to keep fighting his way up the mountain, killing with bullet, bayonet and hand grenade. The battle was raging, reaching a crescendo, then falling into a lull so that he could clearly hear the moans and sobbing of the wounded and dying. Orders were being shouted to tend to the wounded, to re-group and attack again.

The sounds of battle began to increase again and all over the mountain, men were dying on both sides. He kept moving slowly up the mountain from rock to rock. He was killing any human form that appeared in front of him. A figure moved around a rock and he shot him.

A para slapped him on the shoulder and said, "Fucking well done son."

Quickly he moved over to the crumpled Argentine soldier on the floor and saw the pleading in his eyes. He had no pity for the enemy who had invaded a piece of Great Britain and who was trying to kill him, so he drove his bayonet through the soldier's left eye and throat.

He moved forward and jumped down into a hollow, firing his rifle as he went; three Argentine soldiers crumpled to the ground. He drove his bayonet into each one to make sure they were dead.

The sound of battle was reaching a crescendo again. He heard a shuffling sound close by on his right. He turned and an Argentine soldier was on him. He ducked and twisted to his right, drove his bayonet upwards into the soldier's ribs and pulled the trigger at the same time. The man screamed and died.

Then there was a searing pain in his head as a rifle butt struck home. He staggered and bent to one knee. The Argentine soldier kicked him in the ribs and he crumpled to the ground and onto his back. The soldier jumped on top of him and put his hands around his throat. The weight on top of him was immense. A fist began pounding into his left eye and then the big hands were around his throat again. His hands were grabbing at the hands around his throat and his legs were kicking wildly. He summoned all of his remaining strength, heaved his body and twisted. There was a scream and he was now on top of the Argentinian and pounding his face with his right fist until there was no more movement beneath him. He looked around and saw his rifle. He got up off the body, picked up the rifle, pointed it at the motionless soldier and pulled the trigger. Nothing, he was out of bullets, so he drove the bayonet into his heart.

Blowers' body was tossing and turning in convulsions and he sat up suddenly awake. He was wringing wet with sweat and sobbing. He looked around the dark room for an attack to suddenly spring out of a dark corner. He clenched his fists ready to fight.

After a few minutes, he realised that an attack was not coming and he began to regulate his breathing and calm down. He switched on the lamp on the nightstand and sat in bed for a couple of minutes more. He rubbed his face and muttered, "Fuck!" into his hands.

Knowing that he was not going to get any more sleep, Blowers got out of bed and walked into the living room. He sat in the window seat and looked out into the dark morning over Fifth Avenue and Central Park.

10:00am Thursday 13th December

Blowers sat in the window seat drinking fresh orange juice when Tommy wandered into the room still wearing his pyjamas. He turned away from the window and bid his friend a good morning.

Tommy stopped in his tracks. "You look like shit."

"Didn't sleep."

Tommy sighed, "Were you back on that bloody mountain?"

Blowers didn't answer, he just turned away and looked out of the window.

Tommy sighed again and shook his head. He was powerless to help his friend. He was struggling to cope with his own nightmares of being on Mount Longdon, let alone trying to help his best friend.

Blowers downed the remainder of the orange juice and picked up his phone. He pressed three on speed dial.

His call was answered by a young female voice. "Agent Berger, FBI white collar division. How may I assist you?"

"Good morning. Can I please speak to Agent Mike Mulligan?"

"Sure. Who shall I say is calling?"

"Andrew Blowers."

There was a short silence and then a booming voice came on the line "Andy. How are you? It's been a long time. Are you in New York?"

"It's been two years Mike."

"Andy, I was so sorry to hear about Faith. Are you okay?"

"Yes. I'm fine Mike. I'm in New York and I was wondering if you could spare some time to help me on a case I'm working on for Fitch Speciality Insurance."

"I've heard about them. They insure top end jewellery and paintings."

"That's about the size of it, Mike."

"And you'd like to use the FBI's resources to help you find a......"

Blowers cut in, "A diamond tiara insured for five-million pounds."

The agent let out a low whistle. "That's a lot of money."

"You owe me a favour or two Mike and it should lead to an arrest for you."

There was a pause on the line and then the agent said, "Okay. I'm interested."

Blowers smiled to himself. "Good. I'll be at your offices in an hour," and he ended the call.

10:55am Thursday 13th December

Blowers walked into the offices of the FBI's white collar division and told the receptionist that he had an appointment to see agent Mike Mulligan. He was given a visitor's ID badge and told to sit on the sofa opposite the reception desk while agent Mulligan was called.

Five minutes later Mike Mulligan appeared, greeting Blowers in his booming voice. "Andy. It's great to see you," and he embraced Blowers in a bear hug. The agent then let go and announced, "I've been given a new office since you were last here. It's this way."

The receptionist buzzed them through the security door and smiled shyly at Blowers. He smiled back.

Mulligan led Blowers through some double doors, down a corridor and into an open plan office space, which was bustling with agents going about their daily work of solving white collar crime.

The agent pointed to the far-right corner. "That's my office over there."

They walked over to the office and the agent followed Blowers in, closing the door behind him.

Blowers looked around the office. "A big desk, a high-backed leather chair, a conference table and a plasma screen on the wall for video conferencing. You've had a promotion Mike."

The agent waved his hand at the bustling office on the other side of the glass. "The whole kingdom is mine."

Blowers shook the agent's hand. "Congratulations," and then he sat down in the chair opposite the desk.

Mulligan sat down behind the desk and got right down to business. "What help do you need?"

Blowers gave the agent a DVD showing the CCTV footage of the robbery, which he played on the plasma screen and watched in silence. When the footage ended, Mulligan leaned back in his chair and said, "So?"

Blowers told Mulligan everything he had learned about the Baroness, her connection to Thomas Malcom and his theory about the insurance scam. Mulligan listened intently and didn't interrupt. When Blowers had finished, the agent sat in silence for a couple of minutes.

Blowers could see that he was thinking and took the opportunity to get himself a bottle of still water from conference table.

Mulligan got up from his chair and walked over to the office door. Opening it, he shouted, "Agent Jones. Get in here!"

Blowers looked through the office glass and saw a man in his thirties, dressed in a dark grey suit with a navy-blue tie, get up from his desk and walk quickly towards the office.

Mulligan closed the door behind the agent as he entered the office.

"Andy, this is Agent James Jones."

Jones nodded at Blowers, who nodded back.

"Thomas Malcom." Mulligan announced to Jones.

The agent looked at Blowers and then at Mulligan for confirmation that he could divulge information about Malcolm.

Mulligan nodded. "It's okay Jones. Andy is an old friend whose cooperation has led to some important arrests for us over the years. You've heard of the McCraken case?"

"Yes."

"Andy got us the breakthrough on that case and besides, he took a bullet in the shoulder for me on the Dutammie insurance fraud scam four years back. Goes without saying Jones, I trust him implicitly."

Blowers felt slightly embarrassed by what his friend had just said, but tried not to show it.

Jones nodded to Blowers and took a breath. "Okay. He's been on our radar for about six months now. We believe he's trying to become a major player in the New York City area for acquiring precious stones and then quickly moving them on. Unfortunately, we've got nothing concrete on him with which to haul him in."

Blowers spoke. "He's about to move five-million pounds worth of diamonds."

Jones looked at Mulligan who nodded and then asked Blowers, "You think he's broken down the tiara?"

Blowers nodded. "Yes. That's what a smart thief would do."

"When?" Jones asked.

"On or about the nineteenth," Blowers answered.

"Who do we know who can move diamonds worth that amount of money?" Mulligan asked Jones.

"Tommy Ice," Jones said without hesitation and continued, "He's the number one fence in New York City for high quality diamonds and fortunately for us, he's in my pocket."

"You think that Malcom will try to sell the diamonds to Tommy Ice?" Blowers asked.

Mulligan grinned "Oh yeh! You want top dollar for your diamonds, then you go to Tommy Ice."

Blowers looked at Jones who grinned and nodded. "Two years ago, I caught Tommy red handed trying to fence one million dollars in diamonds. In exchange for staying out of prison, he agreed to become my informant. He knows I've let some of his deals slide and he also knows I have a list of all of those deals, and could send him prison at any time. So, he knows he has to play ball when I call him."

Blowers was impressed.

Jones then looked at Mulligan and said, "I'll get on it boss," and he left the office.

Blowers stood up and shook the agent's hand. "Thanks Mike. Keep me updated with what's going on."

The agent smiled. "Sure will Andy."

Blowers was escorted through the office and back to reception, where he handed his visitor's badge back to the smiling receptionist. He winked at her and she blushed.

Back in the office, Agent Jones was on the phone.

"Hello?" a gruff voice answered on the fourth ring.

"Tommy. It's agent Jones. Meet me at the Castle Clinton National Monument in Battery Park in two hours."

There was a pause on the other end of the line.

"Tommy!"

"Okay."

The line went dead and Jones smiled to himself. Finally, he had something concrete to go after Thomas Malcom with.

1:30pm Thursday 13th December

Agent James Jones was cold and getting impatient. He was standing by the Castle Clinton National Monument in Battery Park waiting for Tommy Ice to show up. He pushed his gloved hands deeper into the pockets of his thigh length, woollen coat and he hunched his shoulders against the ice-cold wind which was blowing off the river. He pulled his right hand out of his pocket and pushed the top of the leather glove down to look at his watch. Tommy Ice was late and he could feel his mood getting darker. He turned to look out over the Upper Bay towards New Jersey.

Within seconds, Jones felt a presence behind him. He turned and standing in front of him was a short spectacled man wearing a long parka coat with the hood up.

"You're late, Tommy."

The fence shrugged and pushed his hands deeper into the pockets of his coat. "What do you want man?"

"Thomas Malcom."

Jones saw a little twitch under the fence's right eye. It was his tell and Jones instantly knew that Malcom was planning to move the diamonds to Tommy. He needed confirmation.

"Is he planning to move some high-quality diamonds soon?"

Another twitch.

"Maybe?"

"Are you buying them?"

Another twitch and the agent smiled.

"As soon as the meeting is confirmed to move the diamonds, you will text me the date, time and place. Got it Tommy?"

The fence sighed and looked down at his feet.

"Tommy! You got it?" Jones said forcibly

The fence looked up. "I got it man," and he turned and walked away cursing the FBI agent under his breath.

Jones watched the fence disappear into the crowd and decided he needed to get into the warm indoors, so he headed out of the park towards the Italian coffee shop on Pearl Street. A large cappuccino with extra cream and sugar would go down a treat right now.

As Jones sat down to drink his cappuccino, he took his cell phone out of the right, inside pocket of his suit jacket and dialled Mike Mulligan's desk phone number. The call was answered on the second ring. "Boss, it's Jones. Tommy Ice is moving the diamonds and I've told him to call me immediately when the meeting with Malcom is set."

Mulligan leaned back in his chair and smiled. "Good work. Keep me posted. I'll see you when you get back to the office," and he ended the call.

Jones put his cell phone back into his jacket pocket, lifted the steaming cappuccino to his lips and took a sip. If he successfully recovered the diamonds, it would be a good win for him and boost his chances of becoming Mulligan's deputy.

7:30pm Thursday 13th December

The town car pulled in at the kerbside outside of Blowers' apartment block. Marvin slightly turned to Robyn Fairbanks in the back seat and said, "Please just wait a moment Miss."

Marvin got out of the car into the sleeting winter night, walked around the front of the car to the rear passenger door at the kerbside and opened it.

Robyn got out, shivered and said, "Thank you Marvin," with a warm smile.

Marvin nodded and smiled and closed the door.

Robyn dug into her bag and pulled out her purse.

Marvin held up his hand and shook his head. "Oh no, Miss. I have a standing arrangement with Mr Blowers that his friends are taken care of on his account."

He then reached into the top breast pocket of his suit jacket, pulled out a business card and gave it to Robyn. "I'll be in the neighbor-hood all night, so please call me when you need a ride home."

"Okay. Marvin," and she put the card into her purse, turned, and walked into the lobby of the apartment building.

The concierge looked up from his monitor and saw Robyn walking towards his desk. He smiled. "Good evening, Miss Fairbanks?"

"Yes."

He smiled again. "Please proceed to the elevators on your left and select 'P' for the penthouse. I'll let Mr Blowers know that you're on your way up."

Robyn raised her eyebrows and thought to herself, an insurance investigator who lives in a penthouse of Fifth Avenue and who can donate twenty-five thousand dollars is not your average run of the mill insurance man. There was obviously more to Andrew Blowers than she realised and the thought began to bother her.

As Robyn stepped out of the elevator, Blowers was waiting for her in the doorway of his apartment. "Robyn, I'm glad you came."

She stopped and smiled. She discretely looked Blowers up and down; he looked good in jeans and a cotton checked shirt. Robyn smiled again and gave him a bottle of red wine.

Blowers looked at the label and nodded. "This will go down very nice with dinner." He stepped aside and Robyn entered the apartment. He caught a whiff of her perfume as she passed, Chanel number five, a timeless classic he thought to himself.

Robyn quickly looked around the apartment; a semi-open plan kitchen with a dining table and chairs, two over-size leather corner sofas, a large plasma TV, art on the walls and a framed photograph on the small table beside a lamp. She noticed the window seat and told Blowers that she liked it.

He smiled. "I sit there a lot. Now, can I take your coat?"

Robyn un-buttoned the wool coat and handed it to him.

He hung it on the coat stand by the door and then made his way towards the kitchen, saying loudly, "Please make yourself at home."

She followed Blowers to the kitchen. "I'm a straight-talking girl, so can I ask you a question?"

Blowers turned to face her. "Sure."

"How does a man working in insurance afford all this?" and she waved her right hand at the apartment.

Blowers let out a short laugh. "I'm the best there is and so my fees are high. I bought this apartment ten years ago from a friend of a friend for a good price, and because of that view from the window seat."

Robyn walked over to the window seat, sat down and looked out of the window.

She had been sitting for about a minute when she heard, "Hello. I'm Tommy Bowen, London's premier antiques dealer."

Startled, she turned and stood up. "Robyn Fairbanks, famous urban art photographer."

Tommy grabbed her hand and let out a loud laugh. "I knew I'd like you," he grinned.

Blowers entered the living room from the kitchen. "Good. You've met. Dinner will be ten minutes," and he handed Robyn and Tommy a large glass each of the red wine that Robyn had brought.

At dinner, Robyn was very straightforward in her questioning, "You two look like you've been friends a long time?"

Tommy took a sip of wine and answered, "Since nineteen-eighty-one."

She continued her questions to Tommy. "Where did you meet?"

"In the British Army."

"Which Regiment?"

"Three Para."

Robyn's face was dead pan. "I'm sorry, I don't understand."

Tommy smiled, "Third Battalion, The Parachute Regiment."

"Ahhhh! Paratroopers."

Tommy nodded. "Yes," and noticed that Blowers was beginning to shift in his seat and looked uncomfortable.

The questions kept on coming. "Did you see any action?"

Immediately after asking the question, Robyn noticed that Blowers was now looking at his plate, and was just moving the spaghetti and meatballs around it. She decided to change her line of questioning but Tommy answered the question.

"The Falklands war in nineteen-eighty-two."

"So, you're an antiques dealer Tommy?"

"Among other things," Blowers piped up.

Tommy just raised his glass to his friend and took a large mouthful of wine.

"This is nice wine," he announced trying to change the subject.

Robyn was really interested now. "What other things?"

Tommy shrugged so Blowers answered, "Let's just say that Tommy knows people on both sides of the law and has his fingers in a lot of pies."

Robyn just raised her eyebrows as if to say, "Ah! I see," and took a sip of wine.

Tommy grinned at her and raised his glass. "Here's to free enterprise and making money."

Robyn let out a short laugh. "I like you Tommy Bowen," and she raised her glass.

The conversation for the rest of dinner remained light and after a desert of lemon tart and whipped cream, Blowers, Tommy and Robyn retired to the sofas in the lounge with their coffee. Tommy and Robyn chatted and laughed, and Blowers was content to watch and listen. He noticed Robyn's little traits; the way her eyes sparkled when she laughed and the way she pushed her hair behind her ear when she smiled at him. His heartbeat began to quicken and he began to wonder if he was falling for her.

"Can I please use the bathroom?" Robyn suddenly asked.

Blowers stood up and pointed. "Sure. It's down the corridor and second door on your left."

Robyn stood up, smiled and pushed her hair behind her ear. "Thank you."

Blowers watched her walk down the corridor and Tommy watched his friend. Blowers sat down and took a drink of coffee.

"You've fallen for her Andrew."

"What?

"You heard."

Blowers took another drink of coffee. "I know I have."

Tommy smiled. "Good for you mate. You should take her on a proper date."

Blowers stared at his friend and there was a long minute's silence.

"I'm serious mate. She likes you too. You're a perfect match for each other."

"I know. I'll ask her," and Blowers took another drink of coffee.

"Good!" Tommy said too loudly and then noticed that Robyn was standing by the sofa armrest. "It's nothing love," he said a bit too quickly.

Robyn was confused. "Ohhhhhh kay." She then turned her attention to the painting on the wall behind the sofa.

Blowers turned around and looked up at the wall. "Matchstick men and matchstick cats and dogs."

Robyn was puzzled. "I don't get it."

Blowers laughed and stood up. "It's by L S Lowry. People say he painted matchstick men and matchstick cats and dogs, but I don't see that. I see working class people living in a harsh industrial city facing the daily struggle to feed themselves and their families."

Robyn studied the painting. "I see what you mean. Is it an original?"

Blowers nodded. "Yes."

"Is it worth much?"

Blowers nodded. "A few hundred-thousand pounds."

She smiled at him and pushed some hair behind her ear. "I like it. It's like the artist has done with paint what I do with a camera."

Blowers and Robyn stared at each other for a long few seconds and then she said, "I should go. I've got an early appointment in the morning which I can't be late for."

Blowers smiled. "Okay. I'll call Marvin to come and pick you up," and reached for his phone in his jeans pocket.

Robyn put her hand on his arm to stop him. "Oh! There's no need. I've already called him."

Blowers walked over to the coat stand and took Robyn's coat off the hook. He held it open; she slipped her arms into the sleeves and buttoned it up. She lightly kissed him on the cheek and whispered into his ear, "I had a lovely time and yes, I'd like to go out on a proper date with you."

His heart began to pound.

She pulled away and turned to Tommy. "Please walk with me down to the car Tommy."

Tommy stood up from the sofa. "Certainly love," he said with a wide grin on his face.

In the lobby, Robyn suddenly stopped and asked, "Why does Andy have a photograph of Faith Roberts on the small table beside the lamp?"

Tommy let out a breath and looked Robyn dead in the eyes. "Faith was his wife. They married secretly in San Francisco in two thousand and two. He was head over heels in love with her and his heart was broken when she died."

"So the apartment was his wife's?"

Tommy shook his head. "No, like he told you, he bought it. Years back Andrew did a lot of insurance investigation and recovery work for some very rich people all over the world, and with great success. When he made his first million, he gambled it all on the money markets and won. He quadrupled his money and then invested it very wisely to make even more money. He was already a very rich man before he met Faith and with the money Faith left him in her will, he's now an extremely rich man."

There was a short silence between them and then Tommy said, "I think he's fallen for you."

Robyn pushed her hair behind her ear. "How do you know?"

Tommy smiled. "Love. I've known Andrew since he was a seventeen-year old recruit and I've only seen that puppy dog look on his face once before; when he fell in love with Faith."

Robyn's heartbeat quickened.

Tommy continued, "He has that same look on his face every time he looks at you, and right now he'll be swigging down whiskey to calm his nerves."

Robyn blushed and her heart began to race even faster.

Robyn and Tommy continued their walk through the lobby. Tommy stopped in the doorway and Robyn walked across the sidewalk and got into the waiting town car. The rear passenger window lowered.

"Tommy," Robyn called.

"Yes."

"I think I've fallen for Andy too," and then the window rose.

The car pulled away from the kerb and Tommy smiled to himself. His best friend deserved a second chance at happiness and he might just get it with Robyn Fairbanks, if she is strong enough to cope with his Falklands war demons.

11:30pm 13th December

When Tommy walked into the apartment, he found Blowers drinking whiskey as he had predicted to Robyn. "Calming your nerves?"

Blowers drained the glass and poured himself another large measure. "Yes."

Tommy saw a second glass on the table half filled. He walked over and indicated to it, "For me?"

"Yes." Blowers said a little too sharply.

Tommy instantly recognised the signs of anxiety in his friend. He took a drink of whiskey and decided to mention what Robyn had told him as the car was pulling away from the sidewalk.

"Robyn told me that she's falling for you."

Blowers looked into his glass and said quietly, "I'm falling for her too and feel guilty as hell about it."

Tommy decided to get serious. "Andrew. I've known you since you were a boy soldier and you're my best friend, so here's some best friend advice. Keep all the love you have for Faith in your heart, but move on and live a happy and long life." He took a drink of whiskey and continued, "Tell Robyn how much you loved Faith and that you want to experience that same amount of love with her."

Tommy took another drink of whiskey and looked Blowers straight in the eye. "And you've got to tell her about what happened on Mount Longdon, and about the nightmares because of that bloody night. For god's sake, please, give yourself a chance of having some peace and happiness."

Silent tears were rolling down Blowers' cheeks. He put his glass down on the coffee table, walked around it to Tommy and gave him a hug.

"Thanks mate," he said quietly.

Blowers let go of his friend and walked across the apartment to the corridor and his bedroom.

Tommy heard the bedroom door close and let out a long silent breath. He drained the whiskey glass, put it down on the table and walked towards his bedroom, making his own preparations for dealing with his own nightmares about his experiences on Mount Longdon on the night of eleventh June nineteen-eighty-two.

11:00am Friday 14th December

Tommy Ice was sitting in a window seat in Martin's Coffee Shop on Delancy Street, between Allen Street and Orchard Street. He was on his third espresso. He watched the world go by, anxious that he had not received the telephone call he was waiting for on time. For the twentieth time in the last ten minutes, he picked his cell phone up from the table, looked at the screen and then put it down. He took another sip of coffee and began to drum the fingers of his right hand on the table. He took another sip of coffee and could feel the anxiety building inside him.

He was just about to get up from the table when his phone started buzzing. He answered it, "This is Tommy Ice."

The voice on the other end of the call was smooth and native to New York City. "My name is Thomas Malcom. My associate, who you have met, has told me that you're the man who can move top quality diamonds without asking any questions."

"Sure. I can do that."

"Good. I want to meet at two pm on the eighteenth. I've been told that you never do business in the same place twice, so does that give you enough time to set up a private and secure meeting place?"

"Yes. I'll text you the address twenty-four hours before we meet," and Tommy ended the call.

Agent Jones was sitting in Mike Mulligan's office discussing a new bond fraud case, which had just come in, when his cell phone began to ring. He reached into the right inside pocket of his suit jacket, pulled the phone out and looked at the screen. "It's Tommy Ice," he announced to Mulligan.

He answered the call. "Tommy. I hope it's good news on Thomas Malcom."

Jones listened for a few seconds and then ended the call. Grinning at his boss, he said, "We're on. Malcom's moving the diamonds on the eighteenth and Tommy will let us know the time and place twenty-four hours before the meeting goes down."

Mulligan leaned back in his chair, clasped his hands behind his head and smiled. "Good. I want to nail this son of a bitch. Only scumbags assault women."

Jones nodded, put the cell phone back into his suit jacket pocket and carried on with his appraisal of the new bond fraud case.

11:30am Friday 14th December

Blowers was aware of buzzing coming from the nightstand next to his bed. He opened his eyes and focussed on his phone. He had had a rare night of uninterrupted sleep and he wanted it to continue. The phone kept buzzing. He reached over, picked up the phone and put it to his ear. "Hello," he said sleepily.

"Andy, it's Mike Mulligan. Malcom has contacted Tommy Ice and he's planning to move the diamonds on the eighteenth."

Blowers became fully alert and sat up in bed. "Where are they meeting?"

"We don't know yet Andy. Tommy will let Agent Jones know the time and address twenty-four hours before the meeting."

Blowers let out a silent breath of relief. He now had something to tell Fitch. "Thanks for the update, Mike. Keep me in the loop please."

The agent confirmed that he would and ended the call.

Blowers immediately pressed four on speed dial and got voicemail. He left a message. "Mr Fitch. It's Andrew Blowers. I can confirm that Thomas Malcom stole the diamond tiara. He has broken it down and he's planning to fence the diamonds on the eighteenth. The FBI White Collar Division here in New York now have the lead on the case and will deal with catching Malcom in the act of making the deal. I'll update you further when I know more." He ended the call.

Blowers decided that there was no use in trying to go back to sleep and with phone in hand, he got out of bed and went to the kitchen for breakfast and coffee.

"Good morning," Tommy shouted from the sofa.

Blowers waved an acknowledgement and from the coffee pot warming on the hot-plate, he poured himself a mug. He took a sip and closed his eyes for a moment. He then put the mug down on the counter and sent a text Robyn saying, *Good morning. Would you like to walk in Central Park with me? Meet at Bethesda Fountain at 2pm?* He took another sip of coffee and his phone buzzed. The reply simply said, *Yes.*

Blowers smiled to himself and walked over to the sofa. He sat down and looked at Tommy. "What are you doing today?"

Tommy put his book down beside him on the sofa. "Nothing until I meet Patti at seven o'clock for dinner."

"You called her?"

Tommy grinned. "Yes."

"And she's still speaking to you after the incident in the restaurant the last time you were in New York?"

Tommy was still grinning. "The guy was being an arrogant prick."

"Tommy, you threw red wine over him and cost Patti a producer, and she's still talking to you?"

Tommy began laughing at the memory and when he stopped he said, "At the time, I thought throwing wine over him was better than punching his lights out. Anyhow, it's only taken her six months to calm down, and by the way, you're in the dog house with her now."

Blowers was puzzled. "Why am I in the dog house?"

"She wants to know why you haven't called her and taken her out for lunch."

Blowers took a sip of coffee. "Is she in her office all day?"

"She said she's got meetings all day, so I guess so."

Blowers nodded. "Then I'll go and see her later this afternoon."

Tommy let out a low whistle. "You do that and you'll be on thin ice. You know how she hates being interrupted at work."

Blowers grinned at his friend. "She'll forgive me. She can't help it."

Tommy rolled his eyes, picked up his book and went back to reading.

Blowers took another sip of coffee, leant back into the sofa and closed his eyes.

12:30pm Friday 14th December

Blowers smiled at the receptionist as he walked through the doors of Kent Town Records in the Upper East Side on East Seventy Eighth Street between First Avenue and Second Avenue. He thought to himself that she was a typical Patti employee; brightly dyed hair in an outrageous style, bold dark makeup, nose stud and lip ring.

The receptionist looked up at him. "Can I help you?"

Blowers leaned on the receptionist's desk. "I'm here to see Patti Kent."

The receptionist didn't bother to check the appointment diary on her computer. "Ms Kent is in meetings all day with artists and you're not one of our signed artists," she said with attitude.

Blowers smiled. "Oh! she'll see me. Tell her that Andy Pandy is here to see her."

The receptionist thought for a moment and looked Blowers up and down.

He smiled at her again and raised his eyebrows. She sighed, pressed a button on the console in front of her and spoke into the microphone attached to the earpiece, "Mr Andy Pandy is here to see you Ms Kent."

The receptionist rolled her eyes as if to say, "I told you so," and then her facial expression suddenly changed, as the voice from the intercom said, "Send the bastard up." The receptionist pressed another button on the console and said, "I guess you heard that. You can go right up Mr Pandy."

Blowers said, "Thank you," to the receptionist and walked towards the stairs to his left.

Just before he reached the first step, the receptionist shouted, "What did you do to piss her off?"

Blowers turned and grinned, "I didn't call her when I arrived in New York four days ago."

The receptionist said nothing and went back to her work, and Blowers continued his walk up to Patti Kent's office on the first floor.

Patti saw Blowers walking towards her office through the large glass wall. She got up from behind her desk and as Blowers opened her office door, she ran across the office and jumped into his arms. She planted a big kiss on his right cheek and wriggled down until her feet were back on the floor.

"Andy Pandy," she laughed, "I haven't seen that TV program since we were kids in that hell hole of a children's home in Taunton."

She grabbed Blowers hand, pulled him over to the sofa and flopped down into the soft well-worn leather.

Blowers sat beside her and smiled. "You look great Patti."

She smiled back. "I feel great. My artists are doing great, you're here and I'm having dinner with Tommy tonight."

"I'll not expect him home until sometime tomorrow then," Blowers teased.

Patti grinned showing her perfectly straight white teeth.

Blowers decide to come straight to the point. He took a breath, "You're my oldest friend and I wanted to tell you face to face that I've met someone and fallen in love."

Patti leaned over and gave Blowers a hug. "That's great news, Andrew." Then the questions came tumbling out of her mouth. "Who is she? Where did you meet? How long have you been together? What does she do for a job? Is she rich and famous?" Patti's face turned serious. "If she breaks your heart, I'll hunt the bitch down and kick the shit out of her."

Blowers started laughing and he pulled her close.

When he had finished laughing, he said, "You always did look out for me."

Patti pulled away from him. "I'm being serious."

"I know you are."

"So, who is she?"

Blowers told Patti all about the case he was working on and that he had accidently bumped into Robyn at the Ariana restaurant in Greenwich Village. He told her about their meeting at the fundraiser and about dinner the previous night.

Patti listened intently and when Blowers was finished talking she hugged him and kissed his cheek.

"Robyn Fairbanks," she said shaking her head. "You do like them rich and famous, don't you?"

Blowers shrugged.

She continued, "I know Robyn quite well. I make regular donations to her kids' home charity and I have six of her photos on a wall at home."

Blowers said nothing and Patti playfully punched him on the top of his arm. "I'll still kick the shit out of her if she breaks your heart though."

Blowers just looked at Patti, shook his head and grinned.

For the next hour, Blowers and Patti talked, catching up on each other's news since the last time they met a year ago. She was still the same Patti he had known since they were kids, full of fun but hard as nails.

Blowers looked at his watch and stood up from the sofa. "I'm sorry but I have to go. I'm meeting Robyn in thirty minutes."

Patti got up from the sofa, reached up and kissed him on the lips. "It's great to see you Andrew. Don't stay away too long and please keep in touch."

Blowers hugged her and whispered in her ear, "I will. I promise." He turned and left the office.

Patti watched through the glass wall as Blowers walked towards the stairs. She desperately wanted her oldest friend to be happy after living in darkness for the last two years.

2:00pm Friday 14th December

An ice-cold winter breeze was blowing from the north and Blowers stood with his back to it as he waited beside the Bethesda fountain for Robyn. The collar of his reefer jacket was pulled up around his ears and his gloved hands were pushed deep in his coat pockets. He looked up at the blue winter sky and squinted at its brightness. He then looked around and saw Robyn hurrying towards him. He walked towards her and as she got closer, he saw that she had a worried look on her face.

Robyn hugged him tight and he could feel her shaking.

"Is everything okay?"

She shook her head. "No. I saw Thomas Malcom on the subway. He winked at me and followed me out of the Seventy Second Street station. I think he's been following me here."

Blowers looked around but could not see anyone acting suspiciously. "If he did follow you, then I'm calling in some help."

He pulled his phone out of his coat pocket and pressed three on speed dial. The call was answered on the second ring.

"Mike, it's Andrew. I'm with Robyn Fairbanks at the Bethesda Fountain and she's shaken up. She says she saw Thomas Malcom on the subway and that he followed her out of the Seventy Second Street station."

Blowers listened for a few seconds and then said, "Thank you." He ended the call and put the phone back into his coat pocket.

"Who were you speaking to?"

"A friend. Agent Mike Mulligan at the FBI. He's going to send out a couple of agents to watch your house for a couple of days."

Robyn breathed a small sigh of relief.

Blowers looked Robyn in the eyes. "You're safe with me and I'll have Marvin take you everywhere you need to go, until we get this Thomas Malcom thing sorted out. Okay?"

Robyn took a breath. "Yes."

He smiled at her "Good. Now, shall we walk to O'Neil's Tavern and have a drink?"

Robyn smiled and said, "Let's go." She linked arms with him.

They walked slowly through Central Park, not saying anything but taking in the park's scenery and smiling when their eyes met. Blowers kept a look out for anyone acting suspicious and didn't get any feeling that they were being followed.

Once seated in the tavern, Blowers decided he wanted to know more about Robyn and so he steered the conversation towards her. She told him that the Baroness had had very little to do with her upbringing, and so she spent a lot of her time with her father while she was growing up on the family estate in up-state

New York. She was a 'daddy's girl.' He learned that she graduated top of her class from high school and that she also had a Master of Arts degree and a PhD from Columbia University in Classical Studies.

He wanted to know why she became a photographer and asked, "So, have you always liked photography?

She nodded. "Yes. I was always snapping away when I was a kid. I had this old camera that my dad gave me. I still have it in a box somewhere at home."

"Did you always want to be a photographer?"

She shook her head. "I didn't know what I wanted to do. I liked to read about ancient Greece and ancient Rome so I studied classical studies. I was finishing my dissertation on my PhD and was preparing to pursue a career as a university lecturer when I took the photograph of the basketball players. A friend at college persuaded me to enter it into a competition and unexpectedly I won. That's when I decided that I should try photography as a career."

Blowers listened intently to everything Robyn had to say and learned a lot about her childhood. It was a far cry from his own childhood experiences of not having any family and growing up in a state-run children's home.

After an hour of talking about herself, Robyn asked Blowers about his childhood. He shrugged, "There's nothing really to tell. My parents were killed in a car crash when I was six years old and my Grandma was too ill to look after me, so, I was put in a children's home. It wasn't a very nice place to grow up. I ran away from there when I was sixteen and joined the Paras when I was seventeen. The army became my family and Tommy became my big brother."

The waitress came over to their table and Blowers stopped talking.

"Can I get you folks anything else? More coffee?"

She smiled and stood with pad and pencil at the ready.

Blowers shook his head.

Robyn looked at her watch. "No. Thank you," and the waitress retreated. "I have a meeting at the Luciena at four pm. I'm sorry. I have to go Andrew."

Blowers smiled. "Okay. I'll call Marvin and we'll take you there. "He picked up his phone from the table and pressed five on speed dial.

The call was answered on the first ring. "Mr Blowers, you need a pick up?"

"Yes, please Marvin. From Central Park West by the Sixty Fifth Street Transverse."

"I'm only ten minutes away," and Marvin ended the call.

Blowers looked at Robyn. "Marvin's only ten minutes away. We should make our way out."

They put on their coats and Blowers left a twenty-dollar bill on the table.

They held hands as they walked to the street to be picked up and while they were waiting for the car, they held each other and kissed softly on the lips.

Robyn blushed and pushed some hair behind her ear. Her heart was racing and she felt warm inside.

9:00pm Monday 17th December

Agent James Jones was working late, catching up on some paperwork and was pouring himself his sixth coffee of the day from the coffee pot only two yards away from his desk, when he saw the light blinking on his desk phone. He took a sip of coffee, walked over to his desk and put the mug down. He picked up the phone receiver and pressed the blinking button. He listened to the short voicemail, smiled and cradled the phone.

Agent Mike Mulligan was at home sitting on the sofa with the Monday night football game turned down low. He was reading the file on the most recent bond theft and was getting bored. His cell phone rang and he instantly picked it up from the sofa beside him and answered, "Jones. What can I do for you?"

"Tommy Ice just left me a voicemail. He's meeting Malcom at eight am tomorrow morning in the back room of the Clock Tower Diner on Forty Sixth Street in Long Island City to appraise the diamonds."

Mulligan leaned back into the sofa. "Okay. Put the operation together to lift Malcom. Leave nothing to chance. I want to nail the son of bitch in the act. We'll have a briefing in the office conference room at five am tomorrow morning."

Jones silently punched the air. "You got it boss," and he ended the call.

Mulligan decided he'd had enough of reading the case file, so he reached for the remote and turned up the sound on the forty-eight-inch plasma screen on the wall.

In the kitchen, Mulligan's wife, Tammy, heard the volume on the TV increase and instantly recognised that her husband had stopped working. She got two beers out of the refrigerator and walked over to the sofa. She handed him a beer and snuggled in beside him to watch her team, the New York Jets at the Tennessee Titans.

5:00am Tuesday 18th December

Agent Mike Mulligan looked around the conference room at the seven agents who were all drinking coffee and eating pastries. "Good morning and thanks for coming in so early. Over to you Jones, this is your Operation."

Agent Jones stood up and coughed. He pressed the button on the remote to flash up an image of Thomas Malcom. "This is Thomas Malcom. He's been on our radar for some time and now and we have an opportunity to put him away for a few years. In December twenty-eleven he assaulted Robyn Fairbanks while she was at a fundraiser in London, and stole the diamond tiara she was wearing worth five-million dollars."

The room let out low whistles.

Jones continued, "He's broken the tiara down and at eight am this morning he's going to attempt to move the stones."

Jones pressed the button on the remote and flashed up an image of Tommy Ice. He looked around the room and grinned. "We all know who this is and how valuable he is to us out on the street. Make his arrest look convincing. Cuff him, put him in a vehicle and when the vehicle Malcom is in and out of sight, let him go."

The room nodded.

Jones pressed the button on the remote again and brought up a picture of a diner. "This is the Clock Tower Diner on Forty Sixth Avenue in Long Island City where the deal is going down. It has two entrances, front and back and a fire escape to the back alley."

He pressed the button on the remote again and brought up blue print plans of the block the Diner was in. He pointed with a laser pen. "Me and the boss will go in through the front and Ramirez and Carlisle, I want you to go in through the rear and cover that exit."

Ramirez and Carlisle nodded that they understood.

Jones pointed to the front exit and looked at the only female in the room. "Briggs, I want you to back me and the boss up and cover the front exit."

Briggs gave a thumbs up to show that she understood.

Pointing at the fire escape, he looked at the two agents he had not spoken to. "Talbot, Hernandez, I want you both on the fire escape. One high blocking escape to the roof and one low blocking escape to the alley."

The two agents nodded their agreement.

Mulligan stood up from his chair. "Thanks Jones. Is everyone clear on their assignment?"

The agents nodded, mumbled that they understood and began to get up and leave the room.

Mulligan raised his voice, "Before you go!"

The room stopped moving and fell silent.

"Before you go. Be safe out there. No heroics. I want everyone back here in one piece. Got it?"

The agents nodded, mumbled that they understood and left the room.

7:30am Tuesday 18th December

Tommy Ice nodded to the waitress behind the counter of the Clock Tower Diner as he walked towards the door leading to the back room. He was relaxed. He could spot a fed and a fed vehicle a mile off but as he had made his way to the diner, he didn't see them at all. They were obviously well positioned out of site and that meant that Thomas Malcom wouldn't get scared off.

He entered the back room and switched on the light. The table and two chairs were exactly where he'd asked for them to be positioned, at the very back of the room.

He sat down with his back to the wall, opened his backpack and took out a green felt cloth and laid it across the table. He then took out his eyeglass, tweezers, a leather-bound note book and a pen and put them neatly on the green felt. Finally, he took out a flask of strong unsweetened black coffee and poured himself a cup. He took a sip of the coffee and sat back to wait for Thomas Malcom to arrive.

8:10am Tuesday 18th December 2012

Ten minutes late, Thomas Malcolm opened the door and stepped into the back the room of the Clock Tower Diner.

From behind the table, Tommy Ice studied the man. He was six feet tall, dressed immaculately in a dark blue suit with a black skinny tie, his dark brown hair was neatly combed back and his blue eyes gave his face a cold arrogant look. He indicated to the chair on the other side of the table and said, "Please sit Mr Malcom."

Malcom sat down and stared at Tommy for a long minute. He reached into the pocket of his top coat and pulled out a dark green velvet bag secured by a tightly pulled cord at the top. He loosened the cord and carefully poured the diamonds out onto the green felt.

Tommy Ice drummed his fingers on the table and stared at Malcom, who had not said a word since he had entered the room. Malcom stared back and Tommy began to feel a little uncomfortable.

He selected a diamond using his tweezers, put the eye glass in his right eye and said, "Right, let's get started"

He began to examine the diamond and after a couple of minutes, he put it down to his right on the green felt. He then wrote in the leather-bound note book, looked up at Malcom and smiled thinly.

Malcom just stared at him and didn't speak; his ice cold blue eyes sent a shiver down Tommy's spine and he nervously selected another diamond.

Tommy was just about to start examining the fifth diamond he had selected when the door burst open and two men entered with guns raised shouting, "FBI." He immediately put the eyeglass and tweezers down on the green felt and raised his hands.

Malcom raised his hands, did not speak and did not turn around.

Agent Jones shouted, "Stand up slowly and keep those hands raised."

Tommy Ice and Malcom kept their hands raised and scraping their chairs back, they stood up.

Agents Mulligan and Jones quickly moved forward and holstering their guns, they handcuffed the two men. After reading them their rights they roughly marched them out of the room, through the diner and out onto the sidewalk to two waiting SUVs.

Agent Jones got into the back of the SUV with Tommy and Mike Mulligan got into the driver's seat.

Jones turned to Tommy and said grinning, "We'll wait until the vehicle with Malcom in is out of sight and then I'll un-cuff you so you can go."

"Gee, Thanks," Tommy Ice said sarcastically.

Mulligan turned in his seat and dangled the green velvet bag full of diamonds in front of Tommy. "And we'll be keeping these," he said smugly.

Tommy sighed and said sarcastically, "Gee. Thanks again."

A couple of minutes later, the SUV containing Malcom pulled away from outside of the diner and was soon out of sight. True to his word, Jones un-cuffed the fence, who quickly got out of the vehicle.

Jones also got out of the vehicle and just as Tommy Ice was about to walk away he said loudly, "Have a nice day."

Tommy flipped the FBI agent the finger and walked away down the street in the direction of the East River.

11:00am Tuesday 18th December

Blowers' phone was buzzing on the night stand next to his bed. He groaned and rubbed his eyes into focus. He had had another peaceful night's sleep and had not been transported back into the hell on Mount Longdon. He didn't want that peacefulness to end. His phone stopped buzzing and just as he was about to turn over and go back to sleep, it started buzzing again. He fumbled for the phone and touched 'answer' on the screen. "Hello," he said sleepily.

"Ah. Good. You're awake."

"Mike?"

"Yes Andy, it's me. I'm calling to let you know that we picked up Thomas Malcom this morning while he was in the process of moving the diamonds."

Blowers became instantly awake and sat up in bed. "You've got the diamonds. That's great news."

"Yes. But we'll need to keep them as evidence at Malcom's trial. And before we hand them over to the insurance company, you'll need to get an expert to verify that they are from the tiara. It's a great result Andy, a win for both of us."

Blowers was nodding. "Yes, it is Mike. Thanks. I'll let Fitch know right away."

Blowers was just about to end the call when Mulligan asked, "Tammy wants to know if you'll come over for dinner tomorrow night? Seven Thirty okay?"

"That would be great, Mike. Can I bring a date?"

There was a short silence on the line. "Sure. You're seeing someone? Who is she?"

"Robyn Fairbanks."

There was another short silence from Mulligan's end of the call and then he asked, "The photographer?"

"Yes."

"Wow. Yes. Tammy loves her work," Mulligan said enthusiastically.

"I've got to ask her first, Mike," Blowers said cautiously.

"Sure. See you tomorrow night buddy." and Mulligan ended the call.

Blowers had two calls to make, the first to Fitch and the second to Robyn. But first he would take a shower and have breakfast.

London - 7:00am Tuesday 18th December

Fitch had just said, "Good morning," to Jenny, his Personal Assistant, and was walking through the doors to his office, when the phone in his suit jacket pocket started ringing. He dug the phone out of the pocket and looked at the screen; it was Blowers calling. "Good morning Mr Blowers. I hope you've got some good news for me."

"Yes. It's good news Mr Fitch. The FBI arrested Thomas Malcom this morning while he was attempting to fence the diamonds he'd removed from the tiara."

Fitch closed his eyes and silently pumped the air with his fist. "That is good news, but I sense a 'But' coming."

"There is a 'But'. The FBI will need to keep the diamonds as evidence in Malcom's trial and they won't release them to you when the trial is over, unless an expert has verified them as coming from the tiara."

Fitch's smile was beaming. "That's good news to start the day with Mr Blowers. I understand that the FBI will need to keep the diamonds for a while. I'll have the expert who appraised the tiara for the insurance valuation carry out the verification."

"Okay. I'll let the FBI know and wait to hear further." Blowers ended the call.

Fitch put the phone back into the inside, right pocket of his suit jacket and looked out of his office window at the grey winter clouds rolling in over central London. His mood had brightened and he was suddenly feeling generous. He walked out of his office and stood by his Personal Assistant's desk.

She looked up and smiled, "What can I do for you Mr Fitch?"

Fitch was grinning. "Jenny, take the day off and here's my company credit card. Go and buy yourself something nice for work from Harrods."

The Personal Assistant smiled, stood up and took the card. "Thank you, Mr Fitch. That's very generous. What's the occasion?"

Fitch was still grinning. "Mr Blowers has recovered the diamonds from the Cardenham tiara. It's a good day for the company Jenny, a good day." With that he turned and walked back to his office; leaving his Personal Assistant standing behind her desk and holding the credit card.

Before her boss could change his mind, the Personal Assistant quickly put an out of office message on her phone and email, grabbed her coat and bag and hurried down the corridor towards the lifts. She had some serious shopping to do at her boss' expense and she was going to enjoy every minute of it.

Manhattan, New York City: 11:05am Tuesday 18th December

Blowers went into the kitchen and poured himself a cup of coffee from the pot on the hot plate. He pressed two on speed dial on his phone and the call was answered on the fourth ring.

"Hi Andy. How's your day going so far?"

Blowers' heart beat faster at the sound of Robyn's voice. "Great. I've got some good news."

"What?"

"The FBI arrested Thomas Malcom this morning while he was attempting to fence the diamonds from the tiara."

There was a long pause and then Robyn said, "That is great news." She was relieved and pleased that the FBI would no longer be watching her house, and that she would not have to travel everywhere in the back of Marvin's car.

Blowers took a deep breath. "I was wondering if you would be my date tomorrow night?"

Before he could continue, Robyn interrupted. "Your date to where?"

"I've been asked over to a friend's house for dinner and I would like you to meet him and his wife."

There was a pause and Blowers' heart began to beat faster.

"I'd love to be your date and meet your friends. I'll come over to your place for…."

Blowers cut in, "Dinner is at seven thirty, so drinks here at six?"

Robyn had a big smile on her face. "It's a date. I'll see you at six."

Blowers let out a silent sigh of relief. "I can't wait. I'll see you then." He ended the call.

Blowers leaned against the kitchen counter and took a big gulp of coffee. The mug was shaking in his hands and he began to panic. He hadn't been on a date in the two years that had passed since Faith's death. He began to worry that he would mess everything up and decided he needed some advice. He would call his oldest friend, Patti, later.

1:00pm Tuesday 18th December

For an hour, Robyn had been trying on clothes for her date with Blowers. In the end, she settled for skin tight black jeans, a cream cashmere v-neck top, a pair of black ankle boots and a short black Italian leather jacket. She also decided to wear plain twenty-four-carat gold stud earrings and a twenty-four-carat gold cross and chain. Now she had her phone in her hand and she was staring at the screen. She took a deep breath and pressed nine on speed dial.

"Hello?" Tommy Bowen answered.

"Hi Tommy. It's Robyn. Where are you?"

"Hello Robyn. I'm in Coffee Republic on Seventh Avenue between West Forty Ninth Street and West Fiftieth Street. Is everything okay?"

"Stay there, Tommy. I'm coming over," and she ended the call.

Tommy was confused. He stared at his phone and was wondering what was going on.

1:30pm Tuesday 18th December

Robyn walked into Coffee Republic and was greeted by Tommy, who just held his arms out to say, "What's going on?"

Robyn took off her scarf and gloves and put them on the table, then unbuttoned her coat and put it over the back of the chair. She sat down and looked Tommy in the eye. "Andy has asked me to be his date to dinner at a friend's house tomorrow night."

Tommy began laughing.

"What?" Robyn asked sharply.

When he stopped laughing, he said, "I thought there was an emergency. That's what." He began laughing again.

Robyn waited for Tommy to stop laughing. When he did, she said, "Tommy. This is serious. I'm in love with Andy. This is our first proper date; I'm going to meet some of his friends. All I know is that his parents died and he grew up in a children's home, that he ran away to join the British army, was married to Faith Roberts and is rich."

"That's a lot to know Robyn."

She shook her head. "No it's not. I don't know what makes him, him."

Tommy took a drink from his third cappuccino and looked over the table at Robyn. "You should talk to Andrew about this stuff."

"I know and I will, but please tell me something," she pleaded.

Tommy took another drink.

Robyn pressed him. "You were both paratroopers. Right?"

Tommy instantly didn't like where this conversation was going and the look of concern on his face was obvious to Robyn.

"Please Tommy," she pleaded again.

Tommy shook his head and after a long sigh, he began talking. "Okay. Andrew was seventeen years old when he did his recruit training and I was his Sergeant. He wasn't the usual gun-ho type of recruit. He had a steely calm about him and performed very well in intense pressure situations."

He took a drink of coffee and continued. "Andrew passed selection with flying colours and received his red beret on his eighteenth birthday."

Tommy stopped talking when the waitress came to the table and asked if she could get Robyn anything. She ordered a cappuccino and the waitress left the table.

Robyn smiled at Tommy and asked him to continue his story.

He sighed. "Six months after Andrew passed selection, we were in the Falkland Islands fighting the Argies."

Robyn cut in, "The Argies?"

"Argentina!" Tommy snapped.

"Oh! Sorry."

Tommy went silent and staring into his coffee, he went deep into his private memories of the Falklands war. He became aware of Robyn saying, "Tommy. Tommy!" but it wasn't until she squeezed his hand that he snapped out of the daytime nightmare.

He apologised, "Sorry. We landed at San Carlos bay unopposed and then tabbed all the way across East Falkland in atrocious winter weather."

Robyn frowned. "Tabbed? What's that?"

"Tactical Advance to Battle," Tommy replied and then continued the story. "We slept out in the open in the wind and rain. It was awful but we all knew that we had a job to do, so nobody complained. Andrew started to suffer from trench foot; his feet were a mess but he just kept on walking with the rest of us. He never complained once."

The waitress appeared at the table and put Robyn's cappuccino down in front of her. Robyn smiled and said, "Thank you."

The waitress turned to Tommy. "Can I get you a fresh cup?"

Tommy looked up and smiled. "Yes please."
The waitress smiled, picked up his used cup from the table and walked away.

Robyn squeezed Tommy's hand again. "Please go on."
Tommy nodded. "To capture Port Stanley, the island's capital, a number of surrounding mountains had to be taken first. Our objective was to take Mount Longdon to the North West of the capital. At twenty-hundred hours on the eleventh of June we were ordered to fix bayonets and began our silent attack…"

Robyn interrupted, "What's a silent attack?"

Tommy kept his annoyance at the interruption in check.

"There was no artillery barrage before we attacked. The mountain was a fortress with natural defence positions and the Argies were well dug in. It was pitch black, wet and freezing cold and everything was going well until we reached the base of the mountain. A Corporal stepped on a land mine, he began screaming, the Argies opened fire and all hell broke loose."

The waitress reappeared at the table and put the cappuccino down in front of Tommy. He smiled at her, said, "Thank you," and took a sip.

The waitress walked away to another table and Tommy continued the story. "We ran for the rocks and got organised. We fought inch by inch up the mountain for over ten hours in the dark and freezing cold and suffered terrible casualties. Our company, B Company, suffered such losses that we became an ineffective fighting force and stopped our advance up the mountain. A Company was ordered to come through us and push on to take the summit. It was then that I realised that I hadn't seen Andrew since we ran for the rocks. I didn't know if he was alive or dead."

The pain of telling the story was etched all over Tommy's face and Robyn was starting to feel guilty that she was putting him through this ordeal. But she had to know something about what made Andy the person he is. She had guessed that he would not talk to her about this part of his life, because the memories were too painful. She squeezed Tommy's hand and he managed the faintest of smiles.

"I'm sorry Tommy, but I have to know. I have to know about Andy's darkest fears."

He nodded grimly, took a sip of coffee and continued, "When morning came and we had taken the mountain, the mist began to clear and I started looking for Andrew. The Colour Sergeant was with me and we quickly found him. He was sat in amongst some rocks leaning on his SLR. I had never seen such a sight."

Robyn interrupted, "An SLR is a weapon, right?"

Tommy nodded. "Yes. A self-loading rifle," and he continued, "He'd lost his helmet, he was covered in blood, his SLR was covered in blood from bayonet tip to butt and around him lay five dead Argies. When he looked up his face was a mess. He had a deep cut to his scalp, his nose was broken, he'd lost three front teeth and his left eye was black and blue and nearly closed from the swelling. Both of his hands were black and blue and swollen and he had three broken fingers. He'd literally been gutter fighting for his life using his fists and bayonet."

Tommy shook his head at the memory and silent tears began to roll down his cheeks. He wiped them away with the cuff of his sweater and Robyn squeezed his hand even tighter. Tommy looked at her, his eyes showing nothing but pain.

He continued his story, "Andrew should have received a medal for bravery, but nobody could remember seeing him in the fighting. It's a travesty if you ask me." Tommy kept shaking his head and took a large drink of coffee, which was now cold. "Fighting our way up the mountain wasn't the worst of it. It was the thirty-six hours of artillery bombardment afterwards which was the worst. We couldn't shoot back, so we just dug in, took it and lost some more good lads."

"I'm sorry Tommy, but thank you for telling me this."

Tommy looked at Robyn and half smiled with watery eyes.

"When we arrived in Port Stanley a few days later, Andrew did the best thing I've ever seen a soldier do."

Robyn was intrigued. "What did he do?"

Tommy grinned at the memory. "A little boy about five years old pointed at Andrew and said, Mum look at that soldier's face. Andrew heard him and went over. He bent down and told the boy that you should never back down from bullies, even if it meant getting a face like his. He then took off his beret, put it on the boy's head and told him that he was now a member of the Maroon Machine."

Robyn had tears rolling down her cheeks and searched through her purse for a Kleenex. When the tears were wiped away, she asked, "Does Andrew have nightmares about that night?"

Tommy nodded. "We all do Robyn. We lost a lot of good lads in body and mind. When we arrived back in the UK, we handed in our weapons and were immediately sent out on leave. We were told to forget about it and go and get pissed."

Robyn frowned. "Get pissed?"

"Get drunk Robyn. What should have happened, is that we should have been kept together for a few months and helped to deal with the trauma of what we had done and seen, but instead, we were in the pub drinking ourselves silly. We have never received any help from the army and as a result, the number of Falklands veterans who have committed suicide because of the lack of help has overtaken the number of killed in the conflict."

Silence fell upon the table and Robyn tried to process what she had just heard. Tommy just stared at his coffee cup while shaking his head.

Robyn broke the silence by asking, "Are you okay Tommy?"

Tommy snapped out of his trance and looked up at Robyn. "Sure. I'm okay."

Robyn knew that if she was going to sleep with Blowers, then she would need some advice on how to deal with his nightmares, so she asked, "How did Faith cope with Andy's nightmares?"

"The same way my wife Patti copes. To hold me tight until I fell asleep and then hold me tight again when the nightmares come."

Robyn was surprised. "You're married?"

"Yes."

"And she's called Patti?"

"Yes. Patti Kent. She lives here in New York."

Robyn thought for a moment and asked, "You're married to Patti Kent of Kent Town Records?"

Tommy went to take a drink of coffee and then remembered that it was cold. He put the cup down.

"Do you know her?"

Robyn smiled. "We've been friends for about five years. She helps out with fundraising for the kids' home I help."

Tommy smiled. "That sounds like Patti. She's known Andrew since he was six years old. They looked out for each other in the children's home."

Robyn was being nosey now. "So what's the deal with you and Patti? You live in London and she lives here in New York City. How does that work?"

Tommy grinned. "We love each other but can't live together. Just like Elizabeth Taylor and Richard Burton. We have an arrangement."

"A relationship with benefits."

"Yes."

Tommy then switched the conversation back to his friend. "Are you prepared to hold Andrew tight when the nightmares come?"

Without hesitation Robyn said, "Yes."

Tommy nodded. "They are brutal, so vivid and real. Faith once showed me some bruises she got from Andrew during one of his nightmares. She said it was like he was fighting for his life. Are you willing to go through that?"

Again, without hesitation, she said, "Yes." Then she asked, "Do the nightmares ever go away?"

Tommy shook his head. "No. But they become less frequent because you get used to knowing that someone is there to hold you tight and tell you it's all okay."

Tommy looked at his watch and then stood up quickly, "Shit!" he said a little too loudly.

Robyn was startled, "What?" She also stood up.

"I promised to meet Patti at three-thirty and if I don't leave now I'll be late."

Tommy scraped back his chair and quickly put on his coat, scarf, hat and gloves. "I'm sorry but I have to go."

Robyn smiled. "Of course. I'm very grateful for you telling me all you have and I'm sorry for the pain you went through to tell me."

She walked around the table and gave Tommy a hug.

He returned the hug and whispered in her ear, "Don't break his heart." Then he let go of Robyn, turned and walked out of the coffee shop.

Robyn sat down and the waitress appeared. She looked up, "A cappuccino please."

The waitress smiled and took the used cup way.

Robyn shook her head and typed the battle for Mount Longdon into the search engine on her phone. She scanned the hits on the screen, chose one and began to read.

6:00pm Wednesday 19th December

Robyn arrived exactly on time at Blowers' apartment and as she stepped out of the elevator, Blowers was standing in the doorway to meet her. He stood transfixed. Even dressed casually in skin tight jeans and boots she was so beautiful.

Feeling a little self-conscious at being stared at, Robyn looked herself up and down and said, "What? Too casual?"

Blowers smiled. "No. You're perfect."

Robyn let out a sigh of relief. "Thank you" she said with a beaming smile and entered the apartment.

Blowers closed the door, took Robyn's jacket and hung it on the coat stand. She sat down on the sofa while Blowers went to the drinks cabinet.

"What would you like to drink?" he asked with a smile.

"Bourbon, straight up."

Blowers raised his eyebrows and thought to himself, *Just like Faith.* He poured a generous glass of Jim Beam and then poured himself a glass of Glenturret. He took the glasses over to the sofa, sat down and gave Robyn her drink. She took a large swallow and felt the warmth of the liquor slide down her throat. Blowers watched her and raised his eyebrows again.

She laughed. "I like my liquor neat."

"So it appears." Blowers took a large swallow from his own glass.

They sat for a few minutes in silence and then Robyn asked, "Tell me about your friends I'm about to meet."

Blowers put his glass down on the table. "Mike Mulligan is head of the FBI's white collar division in New York and he arrested Thomas Malcom yesterday. I met Mike six years ago, when I was on a job to find a rare Fender Stratocaster guitar. That's when Mike met his wife Tammy. She was a singer signed to Kent Town records and it was her guitar that was stolen. Mike was already in the middle of a case, which involved a number of valuable musical instruments being stolen all along the eastern seaboard. We worked the case together and we've been friends ever since. We help each other out from time to time."

Robyn took another big swallow from her glass. "Patti Kent and I have been friends for five years." She looked Blowers straight in the eye and he saw that she expected him to tell her about his relationship with Patti.

Blowers picked up his drink and took a large mouthful of whiskey.

"Patti and I have been friends since we were six years old. We grew up in a hell hole of a children's home and looked out for each other. We ran away from the home to London when we were sixteen. Patti got a job in a sleazy record shop, I got a job on a market stall selling fruit and vegetables and we pooled our earnings to rent a one bedroom bedsit. I slept on the sofa."

Robyn listened intently and never took her eyes off Blowers while he was talking.

Blowers took another drink and continued, "We did quite well for ourselves and managed to save enough money to put a deposit down on a small two bedroom flat. But I didn't want to work on a market stall all my life, so I joined the Paras when I was seventeen. That's when I met Tommy and we've been best friends ever since." Blowers took another drink. "Patti's rise in the music industry is well documented so I guess you don't need me to tell you about that."

Robyn smiled. "What is not documented is that Patti's married to Tommy."

Blowers was surprised. "How do you know about that?"

"I had coffee with Tommy yesterday. He told me about Mount Longdon."

Blowers looked down at his glass and swirled the whiskey around. "Oh!" he said quietly.

Robyn leaned over and kissed him very gently on the cheek. "I'm okay with getting to know you a little bit at a time," she whispered into his ear.

Blowers looked at her through watery eyes and smiled softly, "If that's okay with you."

She smiled back and kissed him again on the cheek. "It's okay," she reassured him.

Blowers kissed Robyn softly on the lips.

She closed her eyes. Her heart was beating so fast that she thought it might burst out of her chest. She pulled away and opened her eyes. Her hand was trembling as she raised the glass of bourbon to her lips. "Wow" she said quietly.

As they walked through the lobby of Blowers apartment building, Robyn suddenly stopped.

"What's the matter?" Blowers asked.

"I'm nervous."

Blowers tried to reassure her. "Mike and Tammy are nice people."

Robyn gave a faint smile. "This is our first date as a couple and I'm meeting your friends for the first time. I'm nervous."

All Blowers heard was, "First date as a couple." He smiled at Robyn. "I like that word."

Robyn was puzzled, "What word?"

"Couple."

Robyn looked up into Blowers' dark brown, smiling eyes.

Blowers pulled her close and closed his eyes. A tear rolled down his cheek.

7:30pm Wednesday 19th December

Blowers knocked on the door of the town house and just before the door opened, Robyn squeezed his hand. The door opened and standing before them was a big man, about 60 years old with a friendly face.

"Andy, Robyn. Great to see you. Come on in," Mulligan said loudly.

Blowers and Robyn stepped through the doorway holding hands.

Mulligan took their coats and he was just finishing hanging Robyn's jacket on the hook on the wall, when Tammy Mulligan appeared in the hallway smiling. She held out her hand to Robyn. "Hi. I'm Tammy. It's a pleasure to meet you."

Robyn shook her hand. "I'm Robyn. It's nice to meet you," she said returning the smile.

"Hi Andy," Tammy said as an afterthought and without looking at Blowers.

Mulligan looked at his friend and rolled his eyes.

"Hello Tammy," Blowers replied but got no reply.

Tammy pulled Robyn through the doorway into the living room saying, "Let's get some wine in the kitchen while I finish cooking dinner, and leave the boys to talk sports."

Robyn looked back at Blowers as he shouted, "Have fun."

Mulligan grinned at Blowers, "She's gorgeous."

"I know," Blowers grinned back.

Mulligan put his arm around Blowers shoulder and said, "C'mon into the den. I've got the basketball game on and beers in the cooler."

Twenty minutes later they were sat at the dinner table eating a beautifully prepared meal of honey roast ham, potatoes and vegetables. The conversation was light and very friendly, and Blowers and Robyn guessed that Mulligan had already told his wife about the circumstances they had met under.

Blowers and Robyn exchanged smiling glances as they ate and each time they were caught by Mulligan and Tammy. After exchanging glances for the sixth time, Tammy put her knife and fork down on her plate and said, "Okay you two. You've been sneaking glances at each other all night. Are you a couple?"

Mulligan coughed, "Tammy!"

Robyn smiled. "No. it's okay. This is our first date as a couple."

Blowers looked at Tammy. "You're the first to know, so I guess it's now out there for the world to know."

Tammy beamed at Blowers and clapped her hands excitedly; Mulligan just winked at his friend.

"Well let's celebrate then," Tammy declared. "Mike. Open that good bottle of wine we brought back from France, which we've been saving for a happy occasion."

Mulligan returned to the table five minutes later with four new wine glasses and the bottle of wine in a bucket of ice. He put them down on the table and filled each of the glasses. He gave a full glass to Tammy, Robyn and Blowers and raised his glass. "Here's to you both and the start of what I hope is a long and happy life together."

Robyn smiled at Blowers, who winked back at her and their glasses clinked.

After Dinner when they were all sitting in the lounge drinking coffee and eating after dinner mints, Tammy finally said, "Robyn, I love your work. I'm a big fan."

"Thank you," Robyn said smiling graciously.

Tammy got up from her chair and walked over to the bookcase. She looked back at the table. "I bought a book of your work and I was wondering if you would autograph it for me?"

"Sure. It'll be my pleasure."

Tammy handed Robyn a pen and she wrote on the inside cover, *To my new friend Tammy, thank you for a lovely evening. Robyn XXX.*

Tammy took the book from Robyn and read the inscription out loud. She then excused herself for a minute to the bathroom and took the book with her.

When his wife had left the room, Mulligan turned to Robyn and said, "I told Andy that she's a fan of your work. I'm surprised she was able to keep it inside this long."

Robyn smiled, "Oh! It's okay. It was my pleasure to sign her book. In fact, I'll do better than that and send over a signed original photograph by courier tomorrow morning."

Mulligan grinned, "That'll be great. She'll be your best friend forever after that."

Robyn laughed, "It'll be my pleasure."

When Tammy returned to the living room five minutes later, her eyes were slightly red from wiping tears away. She sat down next to her husband on the sofa and smiled happily at her guests. She thanked Robyn once again for signing her book, who again said it was her pleasure.

The evening continued with laughter and the telling of stories about each other. Robyn was enjoying herself and for the first time since she had been spending time with Blowers, she saw him relaxed, happy and laughing. She glanced at her watch and seeing that it was nearly mid-night, she apologised for having to break up such a great evening, but she must go because she had an early morning video conference with the curator of the Luciena Gallery in Vienna.

Blowers agreed that they should go and he phoned Marvin to pick them up.

The Mulligans were very understanding and thanked them both for coming over.

Since dropping Blowers and Robyn off outside of the Mulligans' house, Marvin had not left the area. He had spent the evening in a diner drinking coffee and doing crossword puzzles. Now five minutes after receiving Blowers call, he stood on the sidewalk in the freezing cold winter night holding the rear door of the town car open for Blowers and Robyn to get in.

The Mulligans waved goodbye and when Robyn saw the front door close, she planted a kiss on Blowers' lips.

Blowers' heart immediately began racing and he returned the kiss with passion. When they came up for air Blowers asked, "Do you really have a morning meeting with a gallery curator from Vienna?"

Robyn grinned. "Yes I do, but I just couldn't wait any longer to have you all to myself," And she kissed Blowers again. Her heart was now beating like a runaway train hurtling down the track with no hope of stopping.

Marvin glanced in the rear-view mirror, saw the couple kissing and smiled to himself.

00:30am Thursday 20th December

Blowers opened the door to his apartment and Robyn pushed past him to get inside first. She turned, grabbed him and pulled him in through the doorway, kicking the door closed as she did so.

Blowers wrapped Robyn in a bear hug and kissed her passionately on the lips. He removed her leather jacket and began to take off her top, while Robyn tried to kick off her boots. When they came up for air, Blowers pulled her towards his bedroom.

Once inside the bedroom, Robyn jumped on the bed and took off her jeans.

Blowers' heartrate was now in overdrive as he took in her slim, athletic figure. He stepped closer to the bed and Robyn began to remove his clothes while kissing him on the lips, cheek, neck and chest. When he was down to his boxer shorts, Robyn slipped under the duvet and took off her bra and knickers.

Blowers grinned, took off his boxer shorts and got into bed. He pulled her close and their legs intertwined.

With their fingers, they gently explored every part of each other's body and kissed long and softly. Robyn then deftly moved on top of Blowers and he slipped easily inside her.

They made love throughout the night, learning what the other liked and eventually at four am, they fell asleep in each other's arms.

10:30am Thursday 20th December

Blowers woke and focused his eyes. The space in the bed beside him was empty but Robyn had left him a note on the pillow. It said that she had gone to her meeting and asked him to meet her for lunch at one pm in Jenny's on Bedford Street, between Barrow Street and Grove Street, in Greenwich Village. Blowers smiled to himself, set the alarm on his phone for eleven-thirty am and sent Robyn a text saying, *see you at 1 XX*. He pulled the duvet up around his ears and went back to sleep for another hour.

As Robyn walked through the front door of her house, her phone buzzed in her purse. She looked at the screen and smiled at the message from Blowers. She did not reply.

Closing the door behind her, she dropped her purse on the floor, kicked off her boots and hung her leather jacket on the coat stand. She then ran upstairs to her bedroom, quickly undressed and walked naked into the bathroom. She turned on the shower taps, let the hot water come through the oversized shower head and stepped into the shower closing the door behind her.

Robyn stood unmoving under the stream of water and let the warmth soak into her body. She closed her eyes and began to recall the night of love making with Blowers. She smiled and began to move her hands gently over her body. She was happy and in love.

12:45pm Thursday 20th December

Blowers walked into Jenny's and found Robyn already seated in a booth waiting for him.

She rose from her chair and gave him a long sensual kiss on the lips.

Blowers' heart was racing again.

They sat down and Blowers asked, "How was your meeting?"

"Great thanks," she said smiling.

A waitress appeared at the table and asked if they were ready to order. Blowers looked up at the waitress and ordered two beers.

Robyn looked across the table at Blowers. "How did you know I wanted a beer?"

"A guess."

"You guessed right."

She then turned to the waitress and told her that they would be ready to order food when she returned with the drinks.

The waitress smiled and walked away.

A minute later the waitress returned with the drinks and had her note pad and pencil at the ready.

Robyn ordered two bacon cheeseburgers with fries and a side order of onion rings.

Blowers shook his head. "How did you know I wanted a bacon cheeseburger and fries?"

Robyn grinned, "I just knew."

The waitress shook her head and said to the table, "I wish me and my old man had what you both have got."

Robyn began laughing and the waitress walked away from the table to give the order to the kitchen.

While they drank their beers and stared over the table at each other, Blowers noticed that Robyn seemed anxious. "Are you okay?" he asked.

She nodded. "Yes, I'm fine, but I have something to tell you."

He felt a knot tighten in his stomach, "what?"

"I have to fly to Vienna tonight to prepare for my exhibition at the Luciena Gallery there."

Blowers breathed a sigh of relief and smiled. "Okay. It's your career and job. You must do what you have to do. I'll see you when the exhibition is over, right?"

Robyn smiled, reached over the table and took hold of Blowers' hand "Of course. I can't wait. I'll be back in New York in two weeks. Will you still be here?" Blowers shook his head. "No. I'm going back to England in a few days."

There was a long moment's silence and then he asked, "How do we make this work?"

Robyn looked Blowers dead in the eyes and in the most serious tone she could muster, she said, "I don't know right now, but I'm going to make it work."

There was another moment's silence and then she said, "I'll move to England if I have to."

Blowers had just started to think about moving permanently to New York and was taken by surprise that Robyn would consider moving to England. "Really?"

Robyn leaned over the table and kissed him by the ear. "Yes. Really," she whispered.

The waitress appeared back at the table with their order. She placed the food down in front of them and asked if she could get them anything else.

Robyn ordered two more beers and grinned at Blowers.

The waitress looked at Blowers who grinned stupidly, raised his bottle to her and took a large mouthful from it. She rolled her eyes and left the table to fetch the drinks.

During the meal, Robyn told Blowers all about her new exhibition in Vienna and how she now wished that it was not taking place over the holidays.

Blowers told her not to worry, that it was okay with him and that it would be all the sweeter when they met again in the New Year.

In truth, both had doubts that they could make their fledgling relationship work.

"Are you coming back to New York in the New Year?" Robyn asked tentively.

Blowers though for a moment. "I thought you might like to join me on my farm in County Durham, and I'll show you the beautiful South Durham countryside in winter."

Robyn took a swallow of beer and smiled, "I'd like that. It's a date."

"That's if we make it out of the bedroom," Blowers teased.

Robyn blushed and took a large swallow of beer. Blowers began laughing and Robyn kicked him under the table.

5:00pm Thursday 20th December

Blowers was lying in Robyn's bed staring into her beautiful, brown eyes. He had expected her bedroom to be quite flowery and girlie with lots of pink, but instead it was very modern and minimalist. The ceiling was painted white with built in lights and the walls were painted a light cream colour. The only items on show were the king size bed, a red leather, high backed chair in the corner near the window and a full-length mirror opposite the bed. A whole wall was taken up with a built-in walk in closet. In fact, all of the interior of her house was very modern and minimalist, which was quite the opposite to his farmhouse cluttered with old and worn furnishings.

Blowers' phone started buzzing and he found it in amongst the tangle of clothes on the wooden bedroom floor. He looked at the screen; Mike Mulligan was calling. "Hello Mike."

"Hi Andy. I'm just calling to tell you that the insurance company's diamond expert has arrived in town and will be looking at the diamonds tomorrow at four thirty."

Blowers looked at Robyn. "At your offices?"

"Yes. A man called Caduggan. Do you know him?"

"No. I'll be there at four o'clock." Blowers pressed 'end call' on the phone's screen.

Robyn raised her eyebrows at the call.

Blowers put the phone down on top of his jeans and laid down on his side to face her.

She gently traced the tattooed parachute wings on the left side of his chest with her right forefinger and read out loud the script below, *Three Para 11th June 1982, Rest in peace my brothers*

Blowers gently moved some hair away from Robyn's forehead and kissed her where the hair had been.

She closed her eyes and smiled.

When she opened them, Blowers said, "Fitch's diamond expert is examining the diamonds at Mike's office tomorrow afternoon."

Robyn said nothing, she just nodded and moved closer to him. She gently stroked his right cheek and softly kissed him on the lips. Blowers responded and their bodies once again entwined.

4:30pm Friday 21st December

Agent Mike Mulligan and Blowers sat opposite Fitch's diamond expert, Mr Caduggan, at the conference table in Mulligan's office. They were waiting for Agent Jones to bring in the diamonds. Mulligan drummed his fingers impatiently on the table while Blowers watched Caduggan clean his glasses.

Caduggan's dark pin-striped suit, white shirt and black tie were immaculate. His thinning, dark hair was slicked back and his pale, blue eyes were ice cold and piercing. Blowers didn't like the man.

Jones entered the office holding the dark green velvet bag containing the diamonds and looked at Mulligan, who nodded towards Caduggan. Jones put the bag down on the green baize laid before Caduggan and left the room, closing the door behind him.

Caduggan pulled a small black leather book out of his briefcase and thumbed through the pages. He stopped about halfway through and put the book down next to the bag of diamonds. He then looked up at Blowers and Mulligan and announced, "Mr Fitch had me examine each diamond in the tiara before he accepted insurance cover." He tapped the book with his glasses. "My notes on each diamond are in this book. We'll see if these are the diamonds from the Cardenham tiara, shall we?"

Blowers nodded and Mulligan grunted.

Caduggan took that as the sign to start the examination. He chose a diamond using his tweezers and gently placed it under the microscope. He looked at the diamond through the microscope, turning it gently and as he did so, and then consulted the notes in the book. He smiled and then placed the diamond on the green baize at the other side of the scope.

Caduggan examined the diamonds for an hour and each time he took a diamond from underneath the microscope, he smiled.

Blowers and Mulligan watched patiently and glanced at each other each time Caduggan smiled.

Blowers became bored and began to daydream about Robyn. He was snapped out of his daydream when Caduggan announced loudly, "Gentlemen, you have recovered all thirty diamonds from the Cardenham tiara."

Blowers let out a sigh of relief and Mulligan slapped the table and said loudly, "You're one hundred percent certain, Mr Caduggan, that they are the diamonds from the tiara?"

Caduggan smiled a thin smile, "Yes."

Mulligan nodded. "Okay. You realise that I cannot release the diamonds until after Thomas Malcolm's trial, and that we'll be calling you as a witness Mr Caduggan."

Caduggan nodded. "I understand."

Mulligan was grinning, "Good. I'll notify the District Attorney that we have our evidence to prosecute Malcolm."

While Mulligan and Caduggan were talking, Blowers had left the conference room. He was on the phone talking to Fitch. "Your expert has just confirmed that all of the diamonds from the tiara have been recovered."

Fitch clenched his right fist and silently punched the air in triumph. "Excellent news Mr Blowers. I need you to come back to London and give me your written report, so that I can begin prosecution proceedings against Baroness Cardenham."

"I'll be there in forty-eight-hours," Blowers confirmed and ended the call. He put his phone back into the left inside pocket of his suit jacket pocket and re-joined Mulligan and Caduggan in the conference room.

Agent Jones was putting the diamonds back into the green, velvet bag and Mulligan and Caduggan were shaking hands.

Blowers reached his hand out to shake Caduggan's. "I've informed Mr Fitch that you've verified that all the diamonds have been recovered."

Caduggan gave a slight bow. "Very good. I'll now take my leave and catch the next available flight back to London." He then turned and left the room without saying another word.

Mulligan quickly walked to the open office door and shouted for an agent to see Caduggan to reception. He then looked at his watch and grinned. "It's happy hour down at O'Hare's. I'll buy you a Guinness Andy. C'mon."

"Sure. Why not," Blowers smiled.

Mulligan put his hand on Blowers' shoulder,

"And you can tell me how much you're missing the gorgeous Robyn Fairbanks," he teased.

"Fuck off!" Blowers grinned back and began walking towards the door.

As they walked through the office, Mulligan shouted, "Jones. We're celebrating. Come and join us for a drink at O'Hare's."

20,000 feet above the Atlantic Ocean - 1:00pm Sunday 23rd December

Tommy had been unusually quiet for the last two days and his face now showed concern.

"Tommy. What's bothering you mate?" Blowers asked.

Tommy looked across at his friend and sighed. "I met with Robyn just before your first date at the Mulligan's house."

"I know. So what!"

"She wanted to know things about you."

Blowers shrugged. "Okay. Like what?"

Tommy looked down at his feet and shifted in his seat. "About your time in the paras."

Blowers felt a knot tighten in his stomach and thought he was about to be sick. He saw the colour drain from his friend's face.

"I told her about Mount Longdon. She said that she was in love with you and wanted to know how to cope with your psychological and emotional scars."

Blowers didn't say anything. He just turned and looked out of the window at the bright blue sky.
Tommy closed his eyes and tried to concentrate on happier things.

They sat for an hour in silence, both deep in their private thoughts.

Tommy broke the silence, "Andrew, I've been thinking about going back to the Falklands."

Blowers stared at his friend "Why? There's nothing but ghosts and bad memories there."

Tommy nodded. "That's why I want to go back, to finally put to rest all of my demons. I've been living with them for far too long and I can't live with them any longer."

Blowers looked out the window again and another silence descended upon the plane.

Twenty minutes later, Tommy piped up, "You should come to Falklands with me. In fact, you, me Patti and Robyn should go. We can put all the horrors of June 1982 to rest and it'll help the girls understand why we are like we are."

Blowers grunted but Tommy persevered, "If you're serious about having a long-term relationship with Robyn, then you owe it to her to help her understand what you go through every night. And maybe it'll also give me and Patti a second chance of being together."

Blowers shook his head slightly and continued looking out of the window. He knew that his friend was talking a lot of sense, but his head was at war with his emotions and they were saying, bad things happened there, don't go back.

After another long silence and an internal battle, Blowers turned to Tommy and said, "Okay. I'm not sure I can handle going back to Mount Longdon but I'll give it a try."

Tommy nodded.

Blowers gave his friend a faint smile. "When we land, I'll speak to John about hiring him to take us down to the Falklands."

Tommy let out a long low breath and a tear began to trickle down his cheek. He looked out of the window and another silence descended upon the two friends.

London - 11:00am Christmas Eve

Blowers stepped out of the lift on the fifth floor at Fitch Speciality Insurance and walked down the corridor.

Fitch's Personal Assistant looked up from her desk and smiled. "Mr Blowers, it's so nice to see you again. I'll let Mr Fitch know that you're here."

Blowers smiled back. "It's nice to see you again Jenny."

The Personal Assistant pressed a button on the speaker phone and smiled again at Blowers.

Blowers nodded his thanks and smiled back. He noticed that she had cut her hair short and that she was wearing a diamond and ruby ring on her left wedding finger.

"Mr Blowers is here."

He heard Fitch say, "Please show him in Jenny."

The Personal Assistant smiled again. "You may go in."

Blowers nodded at her left hand. "That's a nice ring."

The Personal Assistant raised her hand and admired it. "It's beautiful. I got engaged last night."

"Who's the lucky man?" Blowers quizzed.

"Jonathon Coats. He's a criminal lawyer in a top London law firm."

Blowers smiled and said, "Congratulations." He turned, walked four steps and pushed the double mahogany doors to Fitch's office open.

Fitch was standing at a drinks cabinet pouring two glasses of whiskey when Blowers walked into the office. He looked up at Blowers, smiled and put the top on the bottle of Jura single malt. He then picked up the two glasses, walked over to Blowers and handed him a glass. He raised his own glass. "Here's to an excellent result and a Merry Christmas."

The glasses clinked and Blowers took a swallow of the golden liquid. He felt the warmth in his throat, nodded and looked into the glass. "Very nice," he complemented Fitch on his choice of whiskey.

"I had a crate of the stuff flown in from the distillery at Halloween."

Blowers was still looking into his glass. "I prefer Glenturret myself, but this is very nice."

Fitch walked to his desk and sat in the high-backed leather chair.

Blowers took a seat in the soft leather chair on the other side of the desk and just to Fitch's left. He reached down into his leather case, took out a pale blue folder and handed it to Fitch.

Fitch took the folder, opened it and began to read.

Blowers knew that it would take him at least fifteen minutes to read his report, so he settled back into the chair to enjoy the glass of whiskey.

Twenty minutes later, Fitch closed the folder and dropped it onto the red leather, writing mat in front of him on the desk.

Blowers pressed 'send' on the screen of his phone and the text was sent to Robyn.

Fitch smiled. "Everything seems to be in order. A job very well done and a very thorough report Mr Blowers."

Blowers nodded. "Thank you."

"I assume your bank account details have not changed since the last time we did business?" Fitch asked.

"That's correct Mr Fitch."

"Good. I'll have five percent of the tiara's insurance value transferred into your bank account on the twenty-seventh, our first working day after Christmas.

Blowers picked up his leather case and stood up. He buttoned his suit jacket and top coat and reached out his right hand for a hand shake. "That will be fine Mr Fitch," he smiled.

Fitch stood up and firmly shook Blowers hand. "Good. And can I assume that you are now back in the insurance claim investigation business?"

Blowers nodded. "Yes. But I have to advise you that I will be more selective regarding the cases I take on, than I was in the past."

Fitch smiled. "Thank you for the warning."

Blowers turned and started to leave the office when Fitch spoke again, "Oh! There's just one more thing Mr Blowers."

Blowers stopped and turned around to face Fitch.

"I would like you to be present when the police arrest Baroness Cardenham for insurance fraud. I'll have Jenny, contact you with the details."

Blowers nodded, pushed the double doors open and left Fitch's office.

The Personal Assistant looked up at Blowers and smiled. "Can I please check that I have a correct mobile phone number for you?"

Blowers nodded, "Of course," and he reeled off the number.

She looked up. "That's the number I have for you. Thank you for confirming that Mr Blowers."

Blowers started walking down the corridor towards the lifts.

Vienna - 11:00pm Christmas Eve

Robyn switched off the movie on her laptop and picked up her phone. She composed a text which read, *Sitting in hotel suite all alone and wishing u were here. Tommy has your xmas gift. Merry xmas & see u soon. Luv R XX* She pressed 'send' on the screen, sighed and laid down on the bed. She grabbed a pillow, hugged it tightly pretending it was Blowers and closed her eyes.

London - 10:00pm Christmas Eve

Tommy had ordered Blowers to spend Christmas with him, to which Blowers snapped to attention and replied, "Yes Sergeant."

Now they were sitting in Tommy's flat watching Miracle on 34th Street and slowly emptying a bottle of twelve-year-old Glenturret single malt whiskey.

"I love this film," Tommy announced.

Blowers looked at his friend. "Really! A grizzled old fuzz butt like you likes this mushy stuff?"

Tommy smiled. "Yes really. It helps me believe that miracles can happen and that people can live happily ever after."

Blowers rolled his eyes and his phone buzzed. He picked it up off the coffee table and read Robyn's text. He composed a text, which read, *Miss u. Hope u like your xmas gift. Don't open it till 2morrow. Will phone you in the am. Luv Andy.* He pressed 'send' and was about to put the phone back down on the coffee table when it rang.

Blowers answered. "Hello Davy. How are you and the family?"

"We're great Andrew. I'm just letting you know that the XR2 is now ready for sale and to wish you a Merry Christmas."

"That's good Davy and thanks. You have a good Christmas with your family and I'll see you at the farm on the second of January. Merry Christmas."

Davy wished Blowers a Merry Christmas and then ended the call.

Tommy looked over at Blowers. "Is everything okay?"

Blowers responded by raising his glass. "Yes. Merry Christmas Tommy."

Tommy raised his glass. "Merry Christmas mate."

They both took large mouthfuls of whiskey and settled back down to watch what was left of the film.

9:00am Thursday 27th December

Blowers was standing outside of Fitch's offices on Leadenhall Street, waiting for the Insurance CEO and a Chief Inspector of the Met Police to emerge from the building. An icy wind was blowing strongly down the street and Blowers hunched his shoulders and pushed his gloved hands deeper into the pockets of his top coat.

Fitch emerged from the building, closely followed by a tall, slim man in full police uniform. "Let's go and arrest a member of the aristocracy shall we," Fitch shouted happily to Blowers.

The policeman nodded his greeting and Blowers responded by nodding back.

A Bentley pulled in at the kerbside. Fitch's driver got out and opened the rear passenger door.

"Where are we going?" Blowers asked.

Fitch smiled. "Knightsbridge to arrest Baroness Cardenham."

Blowers got into the car and was followed by the policeman.

The driver slammed the door shut and hurried around the car to open the front passenger door for Fitch, who was humming a tune that Blowers didn't know, and which was already getting on his nerves.

The driver checked his mirrors, flicked the indicator stick down and drove the Bentley away from the kerbside into the London traffic.

Blowers looked out the window and almost immediately went into a daydream about Robyn. He had spoken to her on the phone twice a day for the last three days. He closed his eyes and imagined holding her in his arms. He could feel the warm touch of her soft skin and could smell the Chanel Number five perfume she wore.

"Mr Blowers," he heard a voice say. He opened his eyes and found Fitch and the policeman staring at him.

The car had stopped.

"Good, you're with us. Shall we go and arrest a Baroness who has committed insurance fraud?" Fitch said happily.

"Why do I get the feeling you're going to enjoy this?" Blowers said quietly but not quietly enough.

Fitch's face turned serious. "Mr Blowers, there are three types of people in this world that I detest; liars, cheats and bullies. The Baroness is a liar and she deserves what is coming to her; disgrace and hopefully a prison sentence."

There was a pause and Fitch continued sternly, "Now shall we?" And he got out of the front passenger seat and slammed the car door behind him.

Blowers and the policeman looked at each other and got out of the car. The policemen instantly walked over to a Sergeant who was standing shivering next to two police cars. They had a brief conversation and the Chief Inspector walked up the steps to the Baroness's house, closely followed by the Sergeant. Four other police officers got out of the cars and positioned themselves at the bottom of the steps. Satisfied that everyone was in position, the Chief Inspector knocked on the highly polished door.

After a minute's wait, the door opened and the Butler asked, "May I help you?"

The Chief Inspector pushed past the Butler and said, "Yes. Is the Baroness home?" as he stepped into the reception hall.

The Sergeant followed and Blowers and Fitch walked up the steps and entered the house. Blowers nodded to the Butler and Fitch grinned at him.

Baroness Cardenham emerged from the drawing room. "Parkinson. What the bloody hell is all this commotion?" she demanded.

The Chief Inspector spoke, "Baroness Cardenham, I am arresting you for committing insurance fraud against Fitch Speciality Insurance. You do not have to say anything, but it may harm your defence if you do not mention when questioned, something which you later rely on in court. Anything you do say may be given in evidence."

The Baroness looked aghast at Fitch, who just grinned.

"And who the hell are you?" she demanded looking at Blowers.

Blowers couldn't help himself in the face of the Baroness's distaste shown towards him. "I'm the man who's fucking your daughter, Robyn. The daughter who you told your son, Thomas Malcolm, to assault and steal the tiara."

The Baroness was outraged and screamed at Fitch, "This is an outrage. I'll sue your company for every penny you've got."

Fitch smiled. "Oh! I don't think so. You see, the FBI in New York have Thomas Malcolm in their custody. They have a full confession from him and they also have all the diamonds from the tiara."

Blowers watched the colour drain from the Baroness's face and at that moment he felt sorry for Robyn for having a mother like the Baroness. He now knew why Robyn felt no love for her.

The Sergeant took the Baroness firmly by the arm and led her out of the house, down the steps and into one of the waiting police cars.

The Chief Inspector followed and nodded grimly at Blowers and Fitch as he passed them.

Blowers and Fitch left the house, walked down the steps and watched the police cars pull away from the kerbside.

Fitch turned to Blowers and said, "I believe that finally concludes our business, except for the trial. You should find your fee in your bank account by four o'clock today."

He held out his hand and Blowers shook it. Fitch gestured towards his waiting Bentley. "Can I drop you anywhere?"

Blowers nodded. "St Pancras please. It's time to go home."

11:00am Thursday 27th December

Tommy read the text from Blowers, saying that he was going home, and put his phone down on the desk in front of him. He looked up as the bell above the shop door rang.

A man about 6 feet tall, about thirty years old and with short, brown hair entered. He was wearing beige chinos, a navy blazer, a light blue, cotton button down shirt and his brown brogues were highly polished.

As he approached him, Tommy noticed that he walked tall and straight and could see that he was wearing a parachute regiment tie.

Tommy stood up behind the desk. "Can I help you?"

The man smiled. "I've come about the job vacancy advertised in the paper. Are you the owner of the shop?"

Tommy pointed at the chair on the other side of the desk. "Yes. Have a seat."

The man sat down, crossed his right leg over his left and smiled.

"Are you an ex-para?" Tommy asked.

The man nodded. "Yes. I was a Colour Sergeant in two para."

Tommy nodded. "I was a Sergeant in three para."

The man smiled. "Gungey three."

Tommy thought back to how the regiment was nearly always out on exercise and prided itself on being ready for deployment anywhere in the world at any time. Because of this the lads nearly always wore camouflage cream and their state of dress in the barracks usually reflected their readiness for combat and so, the regiment was often called gungey three by the other two para battalions. Tommy was grinning at the memories and then suddenly asked, "See any action?"

"Afghanistan. What about you?"

Tommy looked the man in the eyes. "The Falklands."

The man let out a low whistle. "Mount Longdon?"

"Yes," Tommy said quietly.

"Thank you."

Tommy was puzzled by the comment. "For what?"

The man smiled. "For travelling eight-thousand miles and liberating us in the dead of the South Atlantic winter from Argentina."

Tommy leaned back in his chair.

"You lived in the Falklands when Argentina invaded?"

The man nodded. "Yes. I was five years old when Stanley was liberated." He smiled at the memory and continued, "It was a para who inspired me to join up."

Tommy leant forward, resting his elbows on the edge of the desk. "How so?"

The man was still smiling. "I remember that his face was black and blue and I pointed him out to my mum. Him and another para came over and he told me to always stand up to bullies, even if it meant getting a face like his. Then he put his beret on my head and told me I was now in the maroon machine."

Tommy was dumbstruck, his mouth gaping open.

The man looked at him and frowned, wondering why the shop owner's bottom jaw had dropped.

There was a minute's silence as the two men stared at each other and then the man asked, "Are you okay?"

"Yes," Tommy croaked and then said, "I don't fucking believe it."

The man shifted nervously in his seat. "It's a true story."

Tommy grinned. "I know it's fucking true. I watched it happen. My best friend gave you his beret and I was the other para with him."

"Whhhat?" the man stuttered.

Tommy was still grinning. "Private Andrew Blowers gave you his beret. He's my best friend."

There was another minute's silence as the two men processed that they were meeting again after thirty years.

The man broke the silence. "I'd like to meet him again."

"Maybe you will," Tommy replied as he got up from behind the desk. He knew he couldn't get distracted by the exchange of war stories, so he closed the shop.

"What do you know about antiques?" he asked as he was walking back to the desk.

"Nothing," the man replied. "But I knew nothing about soldiering when I joined up, so I guess I can learn this job from scratch just like I learned how to be a para from scratch. And it's a lot safer than having bullets and RPG's flying at you."

Tommy was impressed by the answer and asked, "What's your name?"

"Mark Stevenson."

Tommy smiled, "You're hired. You start at nine o'clock tomorrow morning."

He stood and held out his right hand for a congratulatory handshake.

Stevenson stood and grinned as he firmly shook Tommy's hand.

Home Farm, Barnard Castle, County Durham - 8:00pm Thursday 27th December

Blowers got out of the taxi and thanked the driver. He watched the taxi turn around in the farmyard and drive away down the lane away from the farm. He turned and began walking towards the farmhouse door. It opened before he reached it.

"Welcome home Mr Blowers," Mrs Pitt beamed.

Blowers gave the old lady a hug. "It's nice to be home Mrs Pitt."

The old housekeeper pushed Blowers into the kitchen and slammed the door shut. "I'll put the kettle on, we'll sit down and have a nice piece of madeira cake and you can tell me all about your trip to New York."

He smiled at the old lady, looked around the kitchen and felt the warmth of the roaring fire on his face. He was happy to be home.

Blowers stuffed a piece of madeira cake into his mouth and took a drink of tea.

"Well?" Mrs Pitt demanded.

He bounced the question back, "Well what?"

"Tell me about New York."

Blowers took another drink of tea. "There's nothing to tell. We caught the thief, the diamonds were found, Fitch doesn't have to pay out any insurance money and the Baroness is probably going to prison for committing insurance fraud. Oh. And my bank account is a little fatter because of a job well done."

He smiled again at his housekeeper and took another drink of tea.

The old lady was not satisfied and she crossed her arms across her chest. "There's something else you're not telling me. I can see it in your face. You look happy."

Blowers shrugged. "What else could there be Mrs Pitt? That's nice cake by the way, please cut me another slice."

She ignored the cake. "Mr Blowers, I have four sons and I know when there is something they are not telling me." She smiled knowingly, "And I know there is something that you're not telling me."

Blowers shook his head and decided there was no point in trying to dodge the subject of Robyn any longer. "I've met someone."

"Who?"

"Robyn Fairbanks."

The housekeeper stared blankly at Blowers and then reached into her apron pocket for her phone.

"What are you doing?" Blowers asked.

"I'm looking her up."

Blowers laughed and reached across the kitchen table for the cake. He cut himself a thick slice and took a big bite.

"I knew it!" the old lady exclaimed.

"You knew what?" Blowers spluttered, his mouth still full of cake.

The old lady put her phone back into her apron pocket. "That she's not some down to earth nobody of a girl. That you'd have to go and get involved again with someone famous."

Blowers pleaded his case, "We just bumped into each other outside of a restaurant."

The housekeeper crossed her arms across her chest again. "Uh hu! And she just happens to be that Baroness's daughter; the one who got attacked and lost the tiara which you were hired to find."

"I'm in love with her." Blowers said quietly.

He began to feel strange inside. It was the first time since Faith's death, that he had openly made his feelings, other than sadness, apparent to his housekeeper. Tears began to roll down his cheeks. "I'm in love with Robyn, Mrs Pitt. I love her." He wiped his eyes with the cuff of his shirt.

The old lady smiled. "Good. You need someone to share your life with. Where is she now? Still in New York?"

Blowers shook his head. "No. She's been in Vienna over Christmas. Tonight, is the last night of her exhibition there. I'll phone her later to see what her travel plans are."

Mrs Pitt got up from her chair and walked around the table to Blowers. She patted him on the shoulder and picked up his mug and plate. "I'll see to the washing up while you get unpacked and settle in for the night."

Blowers wiped another tear away from his cheek, closed his eyes and let the warmth of the fire wash over him.

10:00pm Thursday 27th December

Blowers walked out of the bathroom with only a towel around his waist. His phone began ringing on the dresser and he answered it. "Hi Robyn. I was going to call you in about five minutes."

"Hi Andy. How was your journey home?"

"It was long and tiring. The British rail network is not great. My train from London left forty minutes late. Where are you?"

"I'm on my way to the airport. I'm flying back to New York for a couple of days."

He thought about Robyn's answer for a couple of seconds and then asked, "Where are you going after New York?"

"Well, I thought I might take a vacation in a place called County Durham. It's in North East England you know. And there's a handsome insurance claims investigator who lives there, who I would like to spend some more time with."

Blowers clenched his fist and silently punched the air in celebration. "How long are you planning to stay for?"

"At least two weeks. Is that okay?"

"Sure. Stay longer if you want. I can't wait to see you."

There was a long pause and then Blowers spoke, "Tommy thinks it would be a good idea for me and him to go back to the Falklands and lay all of our ghosts to rest. He suggested that you and Patti come with us. He thinks that it will help us in our relationship and you to understand why I am like I am. What do you think?"

Robyn didn't immediately answer, but when she did she said, "I think Tommy's a good friend and I think it's a good idea."

"You do?"

"Yes."

"Okay then. It will be best to go during the South Atlantic summer. What's your schedule like for February?"

There was a pause while Robyn checked her diary, "It's pretty clear at the moment and if I need to, I'll clear anything I already have arranged."

Blowers was about to speak but Robyn spoke first, "I have to go Andy. I've arrived at the airport. Can we talk about this some more when we see each other?"

"Sure. Have a safe flight."

"Thanks. I love you." And she blew him a kiss down the phone.

Blowers' heart began to beat faster. "I love you too," he whispered and ended the call.

He put the phone down on the bedside table and flopped backwards onto his bed. He closed his eyes and imagined he was holding Robyn in his arms again.

Barnard Castle, County Durham - 9:30am Friday 28th December

Katie Passmoor pushed her daughter, Lizzie, in the pushchair out of the pharmacy on Market Place, and turned right. She stopped at the sound of her name and looked back over her left shoulder. A tall, heavy built, middle-aged man dressed in black was walking towards her.

When the man was close, she asked, "Who are you? What do you want?"

The man smiled, showing two gold teeth. "Katie Passmoor?"

"Yes."

His smile had a sinister edge to it. "Tell Davy his Uncle Paul says hello." He then turned and walked away and did not look back.

A shiver went down Katie's spine and she began to push Lizzie quickly away up the street.

Home Farm, Barnard Castle, County Durham - 10:30am Friday 28th December

Blowers was casting his eye over all the Ford cars which had been restored and updated by Davy. He was very impressed.

"You've done a fantastic job, Davy. I think we're now ready to launch the website and start selling."

Davy didn't hear Blowers; he was on his phone.

Blowers saw the colour drain from Davy's face.

Davy ended the call and put the phone into a hip pocket in his workwear trousers. He looked frightened.

"Is everything okay?" Blowers asked.

"That was Katie on the phone. They've found me."

Blowers put his hands in his jeans pockets and asked, "Who's found you?"

"My family."

Blowers shrugged. "So what?"

Davy looked at the floor and shuffled his feet nervously. "There's something you don't know from when we first met two years ago."

Blowers said nothing and waited for Davy to continue.

Davy looked up at him. "I was working as a runner for the family; you know, at the bottom of the ladder, and I took fifty-thousand pounds from them. I was supposed to deliver it to a back-street bookies, but I was desperate to get away from the family. I had seen my uncle Paul beat up a shop owner for not paying his protection money on time and it made me feel sick. I didn't want any part of it and I saw the money as a chance to get away and start a new life. So I took the money and ran. The first bus that came along just happened to be going to Barnard Castle and you found me about an hour after I had gotten off it.

Blowers thought back to the day he first met Davy. "The blue holdall?"

Davy nodded. "Yes. It was stuffed with money not clothes. The only clothes I had was those I was wearing."

Blowers got serious. "Where's the money now Davy?"

Davy pointed to the white XR3 in the corner of the converted barn.

"It's in the boot of your car. Apart from five hundred pounds, which I spent on new clothes, I've not touched a penny. I've never plucked up the courage to try and give it back."

Blowers walked over to the car and opened the boot. He took out the holdall and opened it. The money was there just as Davy had said. He turned and looked Davy directly in the eyes. "The whole forty nine thousand five hundred is there?"

"Yes," Davy said quietly.

Blowers zipped up the holdall.

"How do you know your family has found you?"

Davy took a deep breath, "Katie said that my uncle Paul stopped her in the street this morning and told her to tell me hello."

Blowers recognised the veiled threat and he put his hand on Davy's shoulder. He sighed.

"You've fucked up mate, but I'm telling you now that everything is going to be okay. Leave it to me. But first I've got to get you, Katie and Lizzy far away from here."

Davy shifted his weight from left leg to right and said quietly, "I'm sorry Andrew."

Blowers put his hand on Davy's shoulder again. "It'll be okay Davy. Call Katie now and tell her to quickly pack a suitcase for you all. Then take the Range Rover, pick them up and bring them here. Do it now and tell Katie to pack light and quickly."

Davy nodded and turned away to get the keys to the Range Rover from the farmhouse.

Blowers took his phone out of his jeans pocket and pressed 8 on speed dial for Captain John Thompson.

The call was answered after two rings. "Hello Mr Blowers. What can I do for you?"

"Hello John. Are you at Farnborough right now?"

"Yes I am. You sound in a bit of a panic, Mr Blowers. Is everything okay?"

"I'm fine John. I need to get my business associate, Davy Passmoor, his wife Katie and their daughter Lizzie off to New York tonight."

"Of course, Mr Blowers. Anything to help. I'll log a flight plan for take-off at twenty- hundred hours tonight. Is that okay?"

"That'll be great John. Thanks. I'll transfer the money for three passengers straight into your bank account," and Blowers ended the call.

Blowers next pressed five on speed dial for Marvin. The call was answered sleepily after the fourth ring.

"Mr Blowers, it's nearly three in the morning. What can I do for you?"

"Hello Marvin. I'm sorry to wake you but it's very important. Can you pick three passengers up at Long Island MacArthur at eight pm New York time and take them to my apartment?"

"Sure, No problem Mr Blowers."

"Great. Thanks Marvin. I'm very grateful." Blowers pressed end on the screen.

Blowers let out a sigh of relief and put his phone back into his jeans pocket. He picked up the holdall, threw it back into the boot of the XR3 and slammed the lid closed. He locked the car.

Now he had to wait for Davy to return with Katie and Lizzie and give them their instructions.

11:45am Friday 28th December

Blowers was sat at the desk in the converted barn reading a text from Captain John Thompson confirming the flight plan, when Davy walked in with Katie, who was carrying a screaming Lizzie. He stood up, walked around the desk and gave Katie and Lizzie a kiss on the cheek.

Lizzie whacked him on the head with her cloth doll.

Blowers looked Katie dead in the eye. "You understand that the three of you are in danger and that you have to leave here now for somewhere safe?"

Katie nodded and Lizzie was still screaming.

"Good." Blowers turned to Davy. "This is what you're going to do. Drive the Range Rover straight to Farnborough air field. Do not stop on the way. The directions are in the satnav. Park in the long stay car park. Then go to the private flights desk and ask for Captain John Thompson. Got it?"

Both Davy and Katie nodded.

Lizzie dropped her doll and began screaming louder.

Davy picked up the doll and gave it back to his daughter, who stopped screaming.

Blowers nodded. "Good. John is flying you out to New York at eight o'clock tonight. When you arrive at Long Island MacArthur Airport there will be a car waiting for you. The driver is called Marvin and he will take you to my apartment in Manhattan. I'll call the building concierge and let him know that you'll be staying there for a while. I'll also arrange for the fridge to be stocked. Have you got all that?"

"Yes," Davy and Katie said together.

Lizzie whacked her mum on the head with the doll.

Blowers nodded. "Right, now this is the last bit. Under the rug in the master bedroom is a floor safe containing twenty-thousand US dollars. The code for the safe is eighteen, twenty-three, zero two. Use the money to buy clothes, toiletries and to enjoy New York City. Now leave. Go."

Katie hugged Blowers and kissed him on the cheek and Lizzie whacked him on the head with the doll again.

Davy shook Blowers hand and said, "I'm sorry for dragging you into this."

Blowers smiled thinly and nodded. "Text me when you've checked in with John Thompson. And don't worry, I'll take care of everything. Now go."

"Okay Andrew. Thanks." Davy took hold of Katie's hand and led her and Lizzie out of the barn.

Blowers shook his head and sighed.

Greenwich Village, New York City: 7:00am Friday 28th December

Robyn was woken up by her phone ringing next to her pillow. She fumbled for it and sleepily said, "Hello."

At the sound of Blowers' voice, she became alert and sat up in bed. She looked at the clock on the night stand. "Andy it's seven am. Why are you calling so early?"

Blowers explained the situation that Davy and his family were in and that they were on their way to New York, where they would be safe until he sorted everything out.

"So what do you want me to do?" Robyn asked.

"Could you stock the fridge and be there at my apartment when they arrive?"

Robyn pushed her hair back from her face. "Sure. What time do they land?"

"Eight pm your time at Long Island MacArthur. And could you take them shopping tomorrow morning?"

"Sure. No problem Andy. I'll take them out to lunch too."

There was a pause and then she asked, "Will you be okay?"

"Yes. I'm about to give Tommy a call. He knows some people who can help."

There was a long, few seconds' silence which Robyn broke, "Please be careful Andy."

"I will Robyn and thank you for helping. You're a star."

"Sure. No problem Andy," and she ended the call.

Robyn put the phone back down next to her pillow and lay down. She closed her eyes and tried to go back to sleep.

Home Farm, Barnard Castle, County Durham – 12:15pm Friday 28th December

Blowers pressed one on speed dial and the call was answered immediately. "Tommy. I need a favour."

"Sure. What is it?"

"Davy's past has caught up with him and I need your help. Can you get a team together?"

There was a pause while Tommy thought. "I'll get back to you within the hour," and he ended the call.

1:00pm Friday 28th December

Blowers' phone buzzed in his pocket. He took it out and answered. "Tommy, have you got a team together?"

Tommy had good news for his friend. "I've got a six-man team together, including me. All former paras and Royal Marine Commandos. It'll cost you five-thousand a man, excluding me."

Blowers let out a long sigh of relief. "When are you leaving?"

Tommy looked at his watch. "We'll be on the road no later than five o'clock."

"Okay. Thanks Tommy. See you soon." Blowers ended the call.

After a couple of minutes of standing in the silence of the barn, Blowers switched off the lights, locked the doors and walked across the farmyard to the house. Opening the door, he shouted, "Mrs Pitt."

The old housekeeper came shuffling into the kitchen. "Yes Mr Blowers. Is everything okay?"

"Davy's in a bit of bother and I've sent him, Katie and Lizzie away to somewhere where they'll be safe."

Mrs Pitt bit her lip and looked worried, so Blowers gave her a hug and reassured her that they would be safe.

"Now Mrs Pitt. We have Tommy and five other guests arriving tonight, so please open the attic room and the shepherd's cottage next door."

The old housekeeper nodded and said, "It'll be nice looking after a house full of boys again." She turned and shuffled away.

Blowers went into the study and sat down in the old recliner. He thought for a moment and then dialled the number for his bank in Zurich.

The call was answered on the third ring. "Hello. Hans Zulle speaking. How may I be of assistance?"

"Mr Zulle, it's Andrew Blowers. How are you today?"

"Ah! Mr Blowers. It's been a while since we heard from you. I'm fine. How are you?"

Blowers ignored the enquiry. "I want to make a withdrawal in the sum of fifty- thousand-five-hundred pounds cash, and I need it delivering to my home tonight."

There was a short pause and then the banker spoke. "That will not be a problem Mr Blowers. There will be the usual three percent charge for the delivery service."

"That's fine Mr Zulle. Thank you," and Blowers pressed end on the phone screen.

5:30pm Friday 28th December

Blowers was just dipping a crust of bread into a bowl of Mr Pitt's homemade vegetable soup, when his phone buzzed on the table beside the bowl. He quickly stuffed the bread into his mouth, chewed, swallowed and answered the phone. "Hello Davy. Are you at Farnborough yet?"

Davy confirmed that they were, that the pilot was looking after them and that everything was okay.

Blowers breathed a sigh of relief. "That's good Davy. Now listen. My girlfriend, Robyn, will be at the apartment to meet you and make sure that you settle in okay. She will have stocked the fridge for you, so you can have a meal. She'll also call round tomorrow morning to take you all shopping and out for lunch."

Davy was surprised. "You have a girlfriend?"

"Yes. She'll probably ask you a lot of questions about me. Tell her anything she wants to know."

Davy was still surprised that Blowers had a girlfriend and tentatively said, "Okay Andrew."

"One final thing Davy."

"What?"

"Give me a telephone number to contact your dad."

There was a long few seconds' silence on the phone and then, "Andrew, I'm....." and Davy tailed off.

"The number Davy," Blowers said assertively

Davy gave Blowers the telephone number and he read it back to him to confirm he'd written it down correctly. He ended the call by again telling Davy not to worry and to have a good time in New York City with his family.

8:30pm Friday 28th December

Two Land Rovers came to a stop in the farmyard and six men got out of them. Tommy walked towards the farmhouse door, which opened before he reached it. Blowers stepped out into the damp, freezing night and the two men embraced. "Thanks for doing this," Blowers said into Tommy's ear.

Tommy pointed back at the Land Rovers. "The lads are just getting their gear. I'll introduce you."

They walked over to the vehicles and Tommy shouted, "Lads, this is former corporal Andrew Blowers of B company, three para. He's my best friend and the man we're here to help." He began pointing. "That's Vince Waite and Terry Cooper, formerly of four-two commando, Royal Marines and veterans of Mount Harriet. That's former Colour Sergeant Mark Stevenson of two para, who's seen action in Afghanistan, and those two are former privates Barry Scully and Ryan Cropper of one para." Tommy then grinned at his friend, "And I'm the sixth man on the team."

Blowers nodded at the men and said gratefully, "Thanks for coming. Bring your kit inside. Mrs Pitt has tea and coffee on the boil and there's homemade cake too."

Blowers left the men gathering their kit and walked back to the farmhouse.

Mrs Pitt appeared in the doorway.

"Tea, coffee and cake please, Mrs Pitt." Blowers smiled.

"The kettle's already on Mr Blowers," and the housekeeper turned away from the doorway and went to the pantry to find some cake.

Blowers met the team at the farmhouse door. "Two of you are in the attic room and the rest of you are in the shepherd's cottage next door."

Tommy piped up, "Me and Mark will take the attic and he pushed past Blowers with Mark Stevenson following closely behind.

Blowers grinned at the rest of the team. "Right. The rest of you follow me next door."

He led the four men next door to the old shepherd's cottage and opened the door. He switched on the light and entered the kitchen. He switched on lights as he walked through the cottage and showed the team to the two bedrooms.

"Get settled in lads and come next door for something to eat and drink. I'll leave the door key on the kitchen table."

The four men nodded and grunted their acknowledgement and as Blowers left the cottage, they began to unpack their kit.

Fifteen minutes later the whole team was gathered in the farmhouse kitchen. The fire in the grate was roaring, tea and coffee was being drunk and homemade fruit cake was being eaten. The conversation was flowing and the laughter was loud.

Mrs Pitt looked around the kitchen and nodded her satisfaction that everyone looked happy and content. She banged an old wooden rolling pin on the kitchen table and the room went quiet. "I'm Mrs Pitt, Mr Blowers' housekeeper and I'll be looking after you while you're staying with us. If you need anything then just ask."

Tommy snapped to attention and saluted. "Yes Sergeant Major."

The old housekeeper put her hands on her hips. "Don't be so cheeky Tommy Bowen. My husband was Regimental Sergeant Major in the Northumberland Fusiliers and I've dealt with worse than you sorry bunch of old fuzz butts in my time," she shouted back.

Tommy felt like a naughty schoolboy who had just been told off by the head teacher. He gave Mrs Pitt a hug, kissed her lightly on the cheek and said, "It's nice to see you again love."

The housekeeper gave Tommy a light playful slap on the cheek and said, "Tommy Bowen. I'm not that kind of girl."

The room laughed and Tommy went to get some more tea and cake.

Blowers joined Tommy at the kitchen table and set about getting to know the other members of the team.

9:30pm Friday 28th December

"Mr Blowers. There's headlights coming down the lane," Mrs Pitt shouted from the kitchen sink.

Blowers joined his housekeeper at the window and looked at his watch. "That'll be the money," he said to himself.

He opened the farmhouse door and walked across the farmyard to the BMW, which had just stopped. He put both hands into his jeans pockets and hunched his shoulders against the freezing cold night. He shivered and the rear passenger door of the car opened.

A tall bald man wearing round, wire-rimmed glasses got out of the car.

Blowers smiled and held out his right hand for a handshake. "Mr Zulle. I didn't expect you to personally deliver the money."

Zulle firmly shook Blowers hand and smiled. "It has been a long time since we last met in Zurich. It's nice to see you Mr Blowers."

"It's nice to see you too. Other than delivering the money, is there another reason you wanted to see me?"

The banker shook his head. "No. I have an appointment in London tomorrow afternoon with Mr Fitch, who I believe you know, and I thought I would take a little detour."

Blowers nodded. "I'm very grateful for the personal service Mr Zulle."

The banker handed Blowers a black leather case. "Fifty thousand five hundred in sterling as you requested."

Blowers took the case, said, "Thank you," and nodded towards the farmhouse. "We have a houseful but you and your driver are welcome to come in for tea, coffee and homemade cake before you head off for London."

Zulle shook his head. "That's very kind but no thank you. I have a plane to catch to London and I would like to get checked into my hotel."

Blowers shook the banker's hand again. "Thank you again."

Zulle got back into the rear passenger seat of the BMW and slammed the door closed. The car turned in the farmyard. Blowers watched it go through the open gates and followed its rear lights down the lane.

When the tail-lights had disappeared, Blowers walked over to the barn, unlocked it and switched on the lights. He put the new case of money in the boot of the XR3 next to Davy's holdall and slammed the lid shut. He sighed and turned to leave the barn to re-join the crowd in the farmhouse kitchen.

10:00pm Friday 28th December

Blowers left the kitchen and went into the study. He closed the door behind him, took his phone out of his jeans pocket and dialled the number Davy had given him.

"Who the fuck is this?" a gruff voice with a deep Geordie accent said on the other end of the call.

"Is that David Passmoor senior? Blowers asked.

"Who the fuck wants to know?"

"My name is not important. I'm a friend of Davy's."

The gruff voice snorted. "That little shit. What the fuck do you want?"

"To set up a meeting for tomorrow night and to settle this once and for all, so Davy can have a normal life with his family and not be looking over his shoulder for the rest of his life."

The gruff voice started laughing and when he stopped, he said, "You have some fucking bollocks calling me like this son."

"Maybe," Blowers said flatly.

"Where the fuck do you suggest we meet?"

Blowers gave the directions, "On the A-six-eight-eight road to Barnard Castle. There's a left turn on a bend to an abandoned farm. I'll mark the turn with a white arrow. It's secluded and away from prying eyes."

The gangster grunted.

Blowers pressed on, "Meet at eight o'clock tomorrow night?"

"We'll be there," the gangster said threateningly and the call ended abruptly.

Blowers let out a long exhale of breath in relief. He pocketed the phone, picked up his laptop and went back into the kitchen. He put the laptop down onto the kitchen table, logged in and got the meeting place up on satellite image.

Tommy walked two steps towards Blowers, saw the satellite image up on the laptop and shouted, "Lads!"

Conversations stopped and Tommy nodded down at the laptop.

The team gathered around and Blowers spoke. "The meeting with the Passmoors is set for twenty-hundred hours tomorrow."

The team studied the satellite image on the screen and started to point to what looked like good areas of cover.

Tommy spoke and pointed on the screen. "We'll park the Land Rovers across that main road and out of sight, here." He moved his finger across the screen and said, "Andrew, you meet here in the open space. That way it won't look like an ambush and the prick will think that you've been watching too many gangster movies."

The team chuckled and Tommy continued, pointing on the screen again. "We'll position ourselves in cover here, here and here." He paused and continued pointing, "there, there and there. You'll be covered from all angles."

The team muttered their approval and each man gave an opinion on the cover available and line of sight to where Blowers would be standing.

Tommy and Blowers listened to each man's opinion and then Tommy spoke. "We'll set out at sixteen-hundred hours, recon the site and settle in for your arrival. You won't know we're there. We'll mic you up with coms before we leave."

"Okay," Blowers agreed.

Blowers noticed Mrs Pitt listening in on the conversation.

She smiled at him and said, "I'll put the kettle on."

1:00am Saturday 29th December

Blowers woke with a start. He rubbed his eyes and realised that his phone was buzzing. He fumbled on the bedside table for the phone and saw that he had two text messages. The first text from Marvin read, *Family safely delivered to your apartment.* The second text message from Robyn read *Davy, Katie and Lizzie arrived. Luv R XX.*

Blowers smiled to himself, relieved that the young Passmoor family were a long way away and were safe. He texted Marvin and Robyn his thanks, put the phone back down on the bedside table and tried to go back to sleep.

8:00am Saturday 29th December

Blowers woke to the smell of a fully cooked English breakfast wafting through the farmhouse.

It had been the usual fitful night's sleep; the nightmares were so real. He was tired, rubbed his eyes and tried to focus. He picked up his phone from the bedside table and noted the time. He stretched and then swung his legs out of bed. He stretched again and sat down on the bed, listening to the sound of voices in the kitchen. He pulled on a pair of old sweat pants and a hoodie and followed the smell of frying bacon down to the kitchen.

Mrs Pitt was happily looking after Tommy and the team, who were sat around the old kitchen table. She saw Blowers and nodded towards the table. "There's tea and coffee in the pots and your breakfast will be ready shortly."

"Thank you, Mrs Pitt," Blowers said wearily and he poured himself a mug of tea. He sat down in the empty space at the table next to Mark Stevenson.

The housekeeper put a plate of bacon, sausage, fried egg, mushrooms, beans and fried bread down in front of Blowers, and in a loud voice said, "Eat up boys, enjoy."

The team acknowledged her by grunting through stuffed mouthfuls of fried food and the old housekeeper smiled to herself.

Tommy spoke up, "Mrs Pitt. On behalf of the lads I'd like to say thank you for looking after us so well last night and this morning."

Again, the team grunted their thanks through mouths stuffed with food.

The old housekeeper beamed and said, "I'll make some more tea and coffee." She hummed zipadeedoodah as she filled the kettle with water from the kitchen tap.

Blowers nudged Mark Stevenson. "She's in her element looking after a house full of lads. She misses her four lads not being at home."

Stevenson nodded and swallowed a mouth full of coffee. "You're a lucky man Mr Blowers, having a housekeeper like Mrs Pitt. This breakfast is delicious," and he stuffed half of a pork sausage into his mouth.

2:00pm Saturday 29th December

Blowers' phone was ringing and he answered it on the fourth ring. "Hi Robyn," he said, walking into the study.

"Good morning Andy. I'm calling to let you know that Davy and his family are fine and that we're about to go out for breakfast before shopping."

"Thanks. I really appreciate you taking the time to look after them," Blowers said gratefully.

"It's my pleasure," Robyn said cheerfully. She continued, "In any case, I'll get the opportunity to quiz Davy and find out more about you."

Blowers laughed. "I thought you might like that."

Robyn started laughing and when she stopped Blowers said, "I'll give you a call when this is all over. I'll book the flight back for Davy, Katie and Lizzie and maybe you can come over with them?"

Blowers held his breath for the answer but without hesitation, she said "Yes. I would like that very much."

He let out a long breath. "Good. I can't wait to see you."

"I can't wait to be with you too Andy," Robyn said softly. "Gotta go Andy, see you soon," and she ended the call.

Blowers' heart was racing at the thought of holding Robyn in his arms again, at feeling her warm breath on his neck and her soft skin against his. He put the phone back into his jeans pocket and sat down in the old recliner. He leaned back and crossed his right leg over his left, put his hands behind his head and closed his eyes. He began to dream of holding Robyn in his arms again.

3:00pm Saturday 29th December

Blowers looked up from chopping logs for the fires in the farmhouse and shepherd's cottage and watched two Land Rovers drive down the lane towards the farm. He leaned on the axe and watched the vehicles park ten feet away from him.

Tommy and the team had decided to recon the meeting site earlier than planned and had returned. They piled out of the vehicles and Blowers walked over to them.

"Is everything okay?"

Tommy grinned. "It's all good Andrew. You've nothing to worry about," and he slapped Blowers on the shoulder. He nodded towards the farmhouse. "Come inside and we'll show you our plan for tonight."

The team followed Tommy into the kitchen and each man either grinned or nodded to Blowers as he walked past him.

Blowers left the wood pile and followed.

When they were all gathered around the kitchen table, Tommy brought up the satellite image of the meeting place on Blowers' laptop. He reiterated that the Land Rovers would be parked and hidden across the other side of the main road. He pointed out that Blowers would be waiting in the open space and pointed on the laptop to where each of the team would be positioned. He looked up at Blowers to make sure he was happy that he would be covered from all angles.

Blowers nodded his approval.

5:00pm Saturday 29th December

Blowers stood in front of the kitchen fire, shaking his head and pointing at the body armour. "Do I really need to wear that thing?"

Tommy's face was stern and he snapped, "Yes. Now put the bloody thing on under your jumper."

Blowers grunted and snatched the body armour from Tommy. He took off his jumper, put on the vest and then put his jumper back on. "It'll be no bloody good if they decide to shoot me in the head," he muttered under his breath.

Tommy grinned. "Now put this receiver in your ear."

He clipped a small pack to the back of Blowers' jeans and ran a tiny mic and wire under his jumper. He clipped the tiny mic to the open neck of Blowers' shirt and adjusting his jumper, he stood back to see how visible the mic was. It was barely visible and in the dark under a coat and scarf it would not be seen at all. Tommy smiled and nodded. "Give it a try."

"Hello," Blowers whispered.

The team all gave a thumbs up and Tommy grinned at his friend.

Blowers smiled back thinly and started to get a dark feeling deep inside himself.

"The very latest in coms and ear piece receivers," Barry Scully said pointing to his right ear. He continued, "I have a friend who knows a guy who just happened to come across a batch of them," he said winking.

Tommy interrupted. "Okay, let's get going. Andrew, you follow closely behind. You need to see everyone's position and be in position when the scumbags arrive."

Blowers nodded and asked, "Is there a safe word I should use if I feel things are about to turn nasty?"

Scully spoke up, "There's no need for one. The mic will pick up any sound from twenty feet away and we will all have night vision, so we'll see any threatening movements any way."

Blowers nodded but still had the dark feeling inside. He was not happy about not having a safe word if everything went to hell.

Tommy tried to reassure his friend. "You're in good hands, Andrew," and he slapped Blowers on the shoulder. He then turned to the team who were all making final checks to their kit and said loudly, "Right lads, let's get to it."

Blowers watched the team file out of the farmhouse door. He picked up his reefer jacket, scarf, gloves and flat cap and followed, smiling at Mrs Pitt who was elbow deep in soapy water at the kitchen sink.

"I'll have tea and coffee ready for when you get back," she said with a slim smile.

Blowers gave the old housekeeper a kiss on the cheek and walked out of the door and across the farmyard to his XR3. He opened the driver's door and got in, buckled the seat belt and started the engine. The engine growled, the wheels spun in the light covering of snow and he sped out of the farmyard and down the lane after the two Land Rovers.

8:10pm Saturday 29th December

Blowers looked at the clock on the car's dashboard. "Fuck" he said quietly to himself. He was beginning to wonder if the Passmoors were going to turn up and then he noticed headlights coming down the old farm track. He got out of the car, went to the boot and opened it. He took out two holdalls, one bigger than the other, and a leather case. He slammed the lid shut and walked to the front of the car where the headlights were still shining. He dropped the bags and case to the ground, shoved his gloved hands deep into his coat pockets and shivered in the freezing cold winter night.

A black Mercedes pulled up about twenty feet away and facing Blowers. He could see four people in the car. They all got out. The biggest of the two men from the back seat shouted, "I hate the fucking country. What the fuck am I doing here?"

The men walked to within ten feet of Blowers, who heard Tommy in his ear say, "picking everything up loud and clear."

"I'm settling Davy's debt," Blowers replied loudly.

The big man stepped forward. "How the fuck do you propose to do that?"

"Are you David Passmoor senior?" Blowers asked.

"Yes. Fucking get on with it."

Blowers picked up the big holdall and threw it to Passmoor's feet. "In there is the original fifty thousand pounds Davy took."

Passmoor did not look at the bag.

Blowers picked up the case and threw it high to Passmoor, who, taken by surprise, only just caught it at chest height. "There's another fifty thousand pounds in that case, call it interest earned."

He then picked up the small holdall and threw it to where the first holdall was on the ground. "In that bag is a further twenty-five thousand pounds as a goodwill payment for you to forget all about Davy and to leave him alone to have a happy life with his family."

"You arrogant bastard," the gangster snarled, "I could kill you right now and walk away one-hundred and twenty-five grand richer."

As he spoke the last word, six red laser beams hit their marks on the four gangsters. "What the fucking hell is this?" Passmoor growled.

The other three gangsters stood still as statues.

"I know yours and your family's reputation, Mr Passmoor and this is my insurance policy for leaving here alive. Before you and your lads even touch your guns, you'll all be dead. If you don't believe me, then go ahead and try it."

The gangsters did not move and Passmoor just glared at Blowers. "You've got some fucking bollocks son," he spat out.

Blowers didn't acknowledge the comment. "Take the money and forget all about Davy."

The man to Passmoor's right reached into the inside of his leather jacket with his right hand and as he was pulling it out, a shot struck home into his right shoulder. The man screamed and crumpled to the floor.

Blowers shouted, "Don't be stupid Mr Passmoor. Take the money and leave alive."

Passmoor glared at Blowers through the lights from the cars' headlights and waved his gloved right hand slightly. Two of his men stepped forward and picked up the bags and case. He pointed at Blowers, "I'll be seeing you."

Blowers shook his head. "No you won't. You don't want a war you can't win, so just forget all about Davy and tonight."

Passmoor ignored Blowers' reply and got into the Mercedes.

The injured gangster screamed at Blowers, "I'm going to fucking kill you."

Another shot struck home in his right thigh and he screamed and fell to the ground again. The other gangsters quickly picked him up and bundled him into the front passenger seat of the Mercedes. They then quickly got into the car, and the driver turned it around and sped away with the tyres spitting up dirt and gravel.

Blowers watched the rear lights disappear down the farm track and then let out a long sigh of relief. He sat down on the bonnet of the XR3 and began to shake. The night's cold cut through him like a knife.

Tommy walked up behind Blowers and put his hand on his shoulder. "That went better than I expected," he quipped.

Another voice piped up, "You don't want a war you can't win," and the team began laughing.

Blowers sighed and said loudly, "Let's get going and out of this cold. Mrs Pitt will be worrying herself silly."

10:00pm Saturday 29th December

Blowers entered the kitchen and shouted, "Lads!" The room fell silent and he continued, "Thanks for coming up here at such short notice. Each of your bank accounts is five-thousand pounds richer."

Barry Scully walked over to Blowers and shook his hand. "It was a pleasure, Mr Blowers. I've not had so much fun since I was in the service. And to be so well looked after by Mrs Pitt too."

Blowers shook Scully's hand and nodded his thanks.

Scully continued, "We're going to set up a perimeter around the farmhouse tonight, just to make sure that those fuckers don't try anything." He grinned, "We'll finish our tea and coffee first though."

Blowers nodded, "I appreciate it Barry."

Scully went back to his position near the fire to continue talking football with Ryan Cooper.

Blowers took a sip of coffee and looking up, caught Mark Stevenson's eye.

Stevenson left his place at the kitchen table and walked over to Blowers. "I just wanted to say thank you."

Blowers was puzzled. "For what?"

"For kicking the Argentines off our islands."

Blowers was taken by surprise and stared at Stevenson for long few seconds.

"You're a Falkland islander? You must have only been five or six years old back in nineteen-eighty-two."

"I was five," Stevenson confirmed.

There was another long, few seconds' silence between the men as they drank their coffee. Stevenson broke the silence, "Here, this belongs to you," and he pulled out of a pocket in his combat trousers, a faded red beret with the Parachute Regiment's winged badge on it.

Blowers stared at the beret and turned it over and over in his hands. It looked old. Then he looked up at Stevenson who smiled. "You gave it to me on the day you liberated Stanley. Your face was all battered and bruised and you said that we must stand up to bullies, even if it meant getting a beat-up face."

Blowers' jaw dropped and then a tear began rolling down his face. He turned the beret over in his hands again, stared at it for a couple of seconds and croaked out a "Thank you." He wiped the tear away with the cuff of his jumper and said, "Thank you," again.

Stevenson smiled. "I wore that beret throughout my tours in Afghanistan. It's seen a lot of action."

Blowers was struggling to keep his emotions in check. He nodded and said, "Excuse me, there's some calls I have to make," and he left the kitchen clutching the old faded beret.

Blowers closed the study door behind him, took his phone out of his jeans pocket and pressed eight on speed dial for Captain John Thompson.

The pilot answered immediately, "Mr Blowers, how are you?"

"I'm fine John. I'd like to book passage for four passengers from Long Island MacArthur to Farnborough in five days' time."

"That'll be on the third of January," the pilot confirmed.

"That's correct. Leaving at nine am?"

"Roger that, Mr Blowers. Four passengers from Long Island Macarthur on the third of January. Departure at oh nine hundred hours."

"Thanks John," and Blowers ended the call.

He then immediately pressed two on speed dial for Robyn. She answered on the second ring.

"Hi Robyn. Are you with Davy?"

"Yes. Marvin's driving us back to your apartment."

"Good. Please tell Davy that his problem here is all sorted out. Finished."

There was a pause in the call and Blowers could here muffled voices. He assumed that Robyn was telling Davy the news.

She came back on the line. "They're very happy. We're going to go out for dinner tonight to celebrate."

"That's nice, have a good night. Listen, I've booked Davy, Katie, Lizzie and you on a private flight back to England. It leaves from Long Island MacArthur at nine am on the third of January."

There was a pause before Robyn said, "That's great Andy. I could use some vacation time and I miss you."

"I miss you too, Robyn. I'll see you soon."

"Okay. See you soon Andy," and she ended the call.

Blowers put the phone into his jeans pocket and sat down in the old recliner. He turned the faded beret over in his hands and memories of the day Port Stanley was liberated came flooding back.

Twenty minutes later, Blowers entered the kitchen just as the team were heading out of the door into the freezing winter night.

"They're going out to set up the perimeter," Tommy explained. "I volunteered to act as runner for tea and coffee throughout the night."

"The cushy job, eh!" Blowers teased.

Tommy just shrugged and grinned.

Blowers yawned and stretched. "Okay. It's been a long stressful day and I'm knackered, so I'm going to go to bed and leave you to it."

He turned and left the kitchen.

"Good night," Tommy called after his friend.

8:00am Sunday 30th December

Tommy and the team were sitting around the table eating breakfast when Blowers walked into the kitchen.

Mrs Pitt was in her element looking after 'her boys'.

"Good morning Andrew," Tommy shouted from across the room.

Blowers just waved his hand and poured himself a mug of black tea. He took a sip and closed his eyes. When he opened them, Barry Scully was standing beside him.

"It was all quiet last night, Mr Blowers. If those scumbags were going to make a move on you they would have done it last night."

Blowers nodded his thanks and took another sip of tea.

Scully slapped him on the back and re-joined the team at the table.

Blowers put the mug of tea down next to the sink and took his reefer jacket off the peg. He buttoned the coat, pulled the collar up around his ears and picking up the mug of tea, he went outside into the snow, which had fallen during the night. He walked over to the barn, the freshly fallen snow crunching under the soles of his boots. He unlocked the doors, opened them and stepped inside. He switched on the lights and looked around at all the restored Ford cars.

Tommy had followed Blowers into the barn. "Impressive," he said from over Blowers' left shoulder.

Blowers did not look round at his friend. "It's all Davy's work. He's a very talented and hardworking mechanic."

Tommy took another look around the barn. He recognised only some of the cars and asked, "So what cars have you got here?"

Blowers pointed them out: "An XR2, two XR3i's, four mark one Escorts, an Escort RS two thousand, two mark one Cortinas, two mark one Granadas and a mark one Capri. All of them are ready for sale."

Tommy recognised the Capri and walked over to it smiling. "I had one of these in black."

He opened the driver's door and got in behind the wheel. He put both hands on the steering wheel and pressed down on the clutch with his left foot. He was still smiling. "Lovely. Brings back good memories," he said to himself.

Blowers had walked over to his desk while Tommy was in the car. He unlocked the cabinet on the wall behind it and took out a key. He walked over to the Capri, reached in through the open door and dangled the key in front of Tommy's nose.

"It's yours. A belated Christmas gift from me and I hope it also makes up for the loss of the writing desk to Lord Watson. Davy rebuilt the engine and converted it to run on unleaded petrol. He put in power steering, upgraded the suspension, shocks and brakes and put in a modern CD stereo. It's also had a re-spray and the interior is also new. Take it for a drive."

Tommy looked up at his friend and grinned. He snatched the key out of his hand and put it in the ignition. He took a breath and turned the key. The engine purred into life first time. He sat for a moment and looked up at Blowers. "Really? It's mine?"

Blowers nodded. "Yes. Now get lost while I fill out the paperwork."

Tommy pressed down on the clutch and selected first gear. He released the handbrake and slowly let the clutch up. He drove the car slowly out of the barn, picked up speed across the snow-covered farmyard and sped out of the gate and down the lane.

Blowers watched the car's rear lights disappear down the lane and he smiled to himself. He closed the barn doors and went over to his desk to complete the paperwork on the Capri.

11:30am Sunday 30th December

From the shelter of the farmhouse doorway, Blowers and Mrs Pitt watched the team load their kit into the two Land Rovers. Tommy and Mark Stevenson were throwing their kit into the boot of the Capri.

Tommy slammed the lid shut and walked over to the farmhouse. He hugged and kissed Mrs Pitt on the cheek and then turned to Blowers. "Thanks for the car mate, she's beautiful," he said gratefully.

"Thanks for putting a team together so quickly and coming up to sort this out for Davy," Blowers responded.

Tommy grinned. "No problem mate. It's been fun."

One by one, the team shook Blowers' hand and said that if he ever needed their help again he was just to call. Each man also said thank you to Mrs Pitt for looking after them so well and kissed her on the cheek.

The old housekeeper began to cry and reached into her apron pocket for a tissue. She wiped her tears away and blew her nose loudly.

Mark Stevenson was the last to say goodbye. "It was nice to meet you again after all these years, Mr Blowers."

Blowers shook Stevenson's hand. "The same here and please keep an eye on that old bugger over there. He has a habit of getting into trouble from time to time."

Stevenson looked back at Tommy and smiled. "I will," and he nodded at the Capri. "It should be a good drive back to London in his new car. Tommy can't stop grinning. He's like the cat who's got the cream."

Blowers smiled and looked past Stevenson. "It's a classic. Enjoy the ride."

Stevenson turned away from Blowers and walked over to the Capri. He got into the front passenger seat and slammed the door shut.

Tommy sounded the horn twice and the car sped out of the farmyard, followed by the two Land Rovers.

Blowers and Mrs Pitt watched the cars disappear down the lane. He put his arm around the old housekeeper, turned her towards the inside of the farmhouse and said, "Put the kettle on, Mrs Pitt. We'll sit beside the fire and have some of that nice banana loaf you baked the other day."

The old housekeeper sniffed, blew her nose loudly again and nodded.

Farnborough Airport - 8:00pm Thursday 3rd January 2013

The customs officer gave Robyn her passport back and in a flat tone said, "Welcome to the United Kingdom, Miss Fairbanks."

Robyn took the passport back and put it into her bag. She smiled at the customs officer and said, "Thank you." She then turned away and dragging her suitcase behind her, she walked out of the arrivals gate to find Davy, Katie and Lizzie.

She saw them instantly; Davy was feeding money into the parking machine and Katie was cradling Lizzie who was asleep with her head resting on her shoulder. She walked over to the family; they all looked tired.

Davy turned away from the machine holding the parking ticket. "All paid for, so now let's go home."

Robyn and the family walked out of the airport terminal and within a couple of minutes they were standing beside the parked Range Rover. Davy pressed the button on the keys and the doors unlocked. He walked around to the back of the car, opened the boot and began loading the luggage.

Robyn got into the back of the car and glanced at Lizzie who was fast asleep in her car seat. She buckled her seatbelt, put her head back on the headrest, closed her eyes and drifted off to sleep.

"I'm looking forward to getting home," Katie said to nobody in particular.

Davy started the engine, turned to his wife and smiled. "Me too sweetheart."

He put the car into drive, released the handbrake and carefully drove out of the parking space. He followed the signs for the exit and said, "In about four hours we'll be home."

Home Farm, Barnard Castle, County Durham - 00:50am Friday 4th January

Davy pulled the Range Rover into the farmyard and stopped it outside of the farmhouse door. The door opened and in six steps Blowers was at the car and opening the rear passenger door.

Robyn got out of the car and jumped into Blowers' arms. Her heart was racing as she kissed him long and passionately on the lips. She did not feel the icy cold wind blowing down the valley and across the farmyard.

Davy got Robyn's suitcase out of the boot of the Range Rover and said loudly, "We'll be off home now. I'll see you later this morning Andrew."

Blowers did not hear him and Davy got back into the car and slammed the door shut. He buckled the seatbelt and drove the car out of the farmyard and down the lane.

Robyn and Blowers came up for breath. "You're shivering. Let's go inside where it's warm," he said while picking up Robyn's suitcase.

They held hands as they walked into the farmhouse and Blowers kicked the old oak door closed behind them. He led her through the kitchen, down the hall, past the study and up the stairs to his bedroom. "This is us," he said quietly.

Robyn looked around the room noticing the king size bed and the antique bedroom furniture. She smiled and said, "It's a nice room." She sat on the bed and then flopped backwards. "I could sleep for a week."

Blowers pointed across the room to another door. "The bathroom's through that door."

Robyn sat up and got off the bed. She walked over to the bathroom and closed the door behind her.

Blowers put Robyn's suitcase next to the wardrobe and then undressed. He pulled on a pair of pyjama bottoms and tee-shirt. He then pulled back the duvet and got into bed.

The toilet flushed and Blowers heard running water in the washbasin. The bathroom door opened and Robyn came out wearing only her tee-shirt and knickers. She got into bed and said softly, "I need to sleep."

Blowers switched off the lamp beside the bed and Robyn wriggled her body up against his. He put his arm around her and gently pulled her closer. Within a minute, Robyn was asleep and Blowers was smiling to himself in the dark.

10:30am Friday 4th January

Robyn opened her eyes, rubbed them and then focused on the room. A bright winter light was streaming through the half open curtains. She listened. Sounds were coming from downstairs. She lay still for a minute, stretched and then got out of bed and went into the bathroom.

After washing her hands and face and tying her hair back into a short ponytail, she pulled on her jeans and went downstairs. A wonderful smell was coming from the kitchen and as she entered, Mrs Pitt turned and smiled. "Pancakes?"

Robyn held out her right hand. "Hi. I'm Robyn."

The old housekeeper lightly shook the offered hand. "I'm Andrew's housekeeper. You can call me Aggie."

Robyn smiled. "I'm pleased to meet you Aggie. And yes please to the pancakes."

She looked around the kitchen and walked over to the roaring kitchen fire. She let the warmth soak into her body for a couple of minutes and then asked, "Where's Andy?"

The old housekeeper smiled. "He's down by the river. He goes there to think. Now my dear, sit down at the table and I'll bring over your pancakes. Tea or coffee?"

"Black coffee please," Robyn sat down at the place set at the table.

11:15am Friday 4th January

Robyn opened the farmhouse door, turned to Mrs Pitt and asked, "How do I get to the river?"

The housekeeper stepped outside into the sunny winter's day and pointed, "Go through the gate, across the field and through the trees. You'll find Andrew sitting on an old fallen tree."

Five minutes later, Robyn found Blowers sitting exactly where Mrs Pitt said he would be. She sat down beside him.

Blowers put his arm around her and she laid her head upon his shoulder.

After a long minute's silence, she said quietly, "It's so peaceful here."

Blowers kissed her on the cheek. "It is. I like to come here to think and try to be at peace with myself." Robyn closed her eyes and listened to the river rushing past.

Blowers smiled; he was happy.

The Falkland Islands - Wednesday 20th February 2013

Captain John Thompson had flown Blowers, Robyn, Tommy and Patti down to the Falkland Islands via Brazil. They had landed two days ago, got settled into a small bed and breakfast in Port Stanley and accepted the hospitality of the locals, who wanted to show their gratitude for liberating them from the Argentines back in nineteen-eighty-two.

Tommy had wanted to visit Mount Longdon immediately upon arrival, but Blowers had made excuses and stalled him.

Now after two days, the two couples and John Thompson stood on the eastern bank of a stream flowing north towards the Murrell River at Furze Bush Pass.

They stood silently for a few minutes. Blowers and Tommy were squeezing Robyn's and Patti's hands. Both men had lost the colour from their cheeks. John Thompson stood silently with his hands in the pockets of his coat waiting for the next move.

"Eton Rifles," Blowers said quietly.

Robyn looked at him. "Sorry, what did you say?"

"Eton Rifles by The Jam, it was the last song I heard before I stepped onto these islands back in eighty-two."

Robyn did not know what to say and just said, "Oh!"

Tommy turned his head and looked at his best friend. "This is where we started our attack from, at eight-fifteen pm on eleventh June nineteen-eighty-two."

Blowers did not answer, he just squeezed Robyn's hand, then let go and took a step forward.

At the bottom of the slopes of the mountain, Blowers and Tommy looked up towards the objective they had known as 'Fly Half'.

Tommy grabbed John Thompson's arm and quietly said, "You'd better come with us. Andrew's got some very personal ghosts to deal with."

The pilot nodded.

The party began to climb the mountain, Tommy steering Patti and John Thompson in the direction of his journey up the mountain on that freezing cold night in June nineteen-eighty-two.

Blowers and Robyn's journey up the mountain was painfully slow. With every step, Blowers could see red and green tracer flying overhead. He could hear the crack of a sniper's bullet being fired, the thwack as it hit home and the screams of the wounded and dying. He was shaking and Robyn squeezed his hand ever tighter. Every now and again Blowers stopped and explained to Robyn what he was doing and experiencing in that place on the mountain on that freezing winter's night. He was shaking and tears rolled down his cheeks. He didn't bother to wipe them away.

Ten minutes after the last stop, Blowers jumped down into a hollow and held out his hand for Robyn to follow him.

She took it and jumped down to join him.

Blowers looked around the area. "This is where I nearly died," he said quietly.

Robyn put her arm around his waist and softly said, "Please tell me what happened."

Blowers took a deep breath and began shaking again. He forced the words out, "I jumped down into this hollow firing my SLR and killed three Argentine marines right there in front of me. To make sure they were dead I drove my bayonet into each of their hearts. I then heard shuffling close by over there on my right. I turned and an Argentine marine was on me. I ducked and twisted to my right, drove my bayonet upwards into his ribs and pulled the trigger. He screamed and died."

Blowers was sobbing now and shaking uncontrollably.

Robyn hugged him tightly and he squeezed her back, letting the tears flow freely.

After five minutes, Blowers had composed himself to when he could speak again. Robyn looked lovingly into his watery eyes and asked, "Are you okay? Can you continue?"

Blowers nodded and sniffed. "I next remember a searing pain in my head and a warmth flowing down the side of my face. I staggered and went down on one knee right there by that rock. An Argentine marine then kicked me in the ribs and I fell onto my back. He jumped on top of me and began to strangle me. He then pounded my left eye with his fist and then began strangling me again. I knew I was going to die if I did not summon up every ounce of strength I had left, so I heaved my body upwards and twisted. I was now on top of him and I pounded his face until I felt no movement beneath me."

He knew he was very close to the end of the story, so he took a deep breath and carried on, "I was exhausted. I got up off the marine, found my SLR and tried to shoot him. I was out of bullets so I drove the bayonet into his chest three times."

Blowers shook his head and the tears began flowing again.

Robyn squeezed him tightly.

After a few minutes, Blowers disentangled himself from Robyn, sat down on a rock and continued with the final part of his story. "Morning was about to break and I could hear the fighting waning. I was exhausted, so I just sat down here on this rock and leaned on my SLR for support. This is where Tommy and the Colour Sergeant found me, surrounded by five dead Argentine marines."

Robyn looked around the area of the mountain she was standing in and tried to imagine what it was like for an eighteen-year-old soldier fighting for his life in the freezing cold of a South Atlantic winter night. She could not imagine. She looked at Blowers who sat slumped forward on the rock he was found sitting on the morning after the battle, staring at the ground. She walked over to him, sat down beside him and linked her arm through his. "I love you," she said quietly.

Blowers sighed, smiled at her through watery eyes and it felt to him like a weight being lifted off him. His healing process had just begun.

Printed in Great
Britain
by Amazon